SILENCE OF THE

P9-DUK-340

DATE DUE

MY 12 '95			
MY 26 '95			
JY 20 '95			
NO 27 '95			
DE 20 '96			
MR 2 0 '00			
OC 22 '03			

DEMCO 38-296

THE
SILENCE
OF
THE
LLANO

THE
SILENCE
OF
THE
LLANO

short stories

Rudolfo A. Anaya

A TQS BOOK

TQS PUBLICATIONS
A Division of Tonatiuh-Quinto Sol International, Inc.

TQS PUBLICATIONS

A Division of Tonatiuh-Quinto Sol International, Inc.
POST OFFICE BOX 9275   BERKELEY, CALIFORNIA 94709

CONTENTS

He hitched the wagon and made the long drive into the village, arriving at the break of light to rouse the old partera from her sleep. For many years the old woman had delivered the babies born in the village or in the nearby ranches, and now, as he explained what had happened and the need to hurry, she nodded solemnly. She packed the things she would need, then kneeled at her altar and made the sign of the cross.

THE
SILENCE
OF
THE
LLANO

I

His name was Rafael, and he lived on a ranch in the lonely and desolate llano. He had no close neighbors; the nearest home was many miles away on the dirt road which led to the small village of Las Animas. Rafael went to the village only once a month for provisions, quickly buying what he needed, never stopping to talk with the other rancheros who came to the general store to buy what they needed and to swap stories.

Long ago, the friends his parents had known stopped visiting Rafael. The people whispered that the silence of the llano had taken Rafael's soul, and they respected his right to live alone. They knew the hurt he suffered. The dirt road which led from the village to his ranch was overgrown with mesquite bushes and the sparse

grasses of the flat country. The dry plain was a
cruel expanse broken only by gullies and mesas
spotted with juniper and piñon trees.

The people of this country knew the loneliness of the llano; they realized that sometimes
the silence of the endless plain grew so heavy and
oppressive it became unbearable. When a man
heard voices in the wind of the llano, he knew it
was time to ride to the village just to listen to the
voices of other men. They knew that after many
days of riding alone under the burning sun and
listening only to the moaning wind, a man could
begin to talk to himself. When a man heard the
sound of his voice in the silence, he sensed the
danger of his lonely existence. Then he would
ride to his ranch, saddle a fresh horse, explain to
his wife that he needed something in the village,
a plug of tobacco, perhaps a new knife, or a jar of
salve for deworming the cattle. It was a pretense,
in his heart each man knew he went to break the
hold of the silence.

Las Animas was only a mud-cluster of homes,
a general store, a small church, a sparse gathering
of life in the wide plain. The old men of the village sat on a bench in front of the store, shaded
by the portal in summer, warmed by the southern
sun in winter. They talked about the weather, the
dry spells they had known as rancheros on the
llano, the bad winters, the price of cattle and
sheep. They sniffed the air and predicted the
coming of the summer rains, and they discussed
the news of the latest politics at the county seat.

The men who rode in listened attentively,
nodding as they listened to the soft, full words of
the old men, rocking back and forth on their
boots, taking pleasure in the sounds they heard.

Sometimes one of them would buy a bottle and they would drink and laugh and slap each other on the back as friends will do. Then, fortified by this simple act, each man returned home to share what he had heard with his family. Each would lie with his wife in the warm bed of night, the wind moaning softly outside, and he would tell the stories he had heard: so and so had died, someone they knew had married and moved away, the current price of wool and yearlings. The news of a world so far away was like a dream. The wife listened and was also fortified for the long days of loneliness. In adjoining rooms the children listened and heard the muffled sounds of the words and laughter of the father and mother. Later they would speak the words they heard as they cared for the ranch animals or helped the mother in the house, and in this way their own world grew and expanded.

Rafael knew well the silence of the llano. He was only fifteen when his father and mother died in a sudden, deadly blizzard which caught them on the road to Las Animas. Days later, when finally Rafael could break the snowdrifts for the horse, he had found them. There at La Angostura, where the road followed the edge of a deep arroyo, the horses had bolted or the wagon had slipped in the snow and ice. The wagon had overturned, pinning his father beneath the massive weight. His mother lay beside him, holding him in her arms. His father had been a strong man, he could have made a shelter, burned the wagon to survive the night, but pinned as he was he had been helpless and his wife could not lift the weight of the huge wagon. She had held him in her arms, covered both of them with her coat and blankets, but that night they had frozen. It took Rafael all day to dig graves in the frozen ground, then he buried them there, high on the slope of La Angostura where the summer rains would not wash away the graves.

That winter was cruel in other ways. Blizzards swept in from the north and piled the snow drifts around the house. Snow and wind drove the cattle against the fences where they huddled together and suffocated as the drifts grew. Rafael worked night and day to try to save his animals, and still he lost half of the herd to the punishing storms. Only the constant work and simple words and phrases he remembered his father and mother speaking kept Rafael alive that winter.

Spring came, the land thawed, the calves were born, and the work of a new season began. But first Rafael rode to the place where he had buried his parents. He placed a cross over their common grave, then he rode to the village of Las Animas and told the priest what had happened. The people gathered and a Mass for the dead was prayed. The women cried and the men slapped Rafael on the back and offered their condolences. All grieved, they had lost good friends, but they knew that was the way of death on the llano, swift and sudden. Now the work of spring was on them. The herds had to be rebuilt after the terrible winter, fences needed mending. As the people returned to their work they forgot about Rafael.

But one woman in the village did not forget. She saw the loneliness in his face, she sensed the pain he felt at the loss of his parents. At first she felt pity when she saw him standing in the church alone, then she felt love. She knew about loneliness, she had lost her parents when she was very young and she had lived most of her life in a room at the back of the small adobe church. Her work was to keep the church clean and to take care of the old priest. It was this young woman who reached out and spoke to Rafael, and when he heard her voice he remembered the danger of the silence of the llano. He smiled and spoke to her. Thereafter, on Sundays he began to ride in to visit her. They would sit together during the Mass, and after that they would walk together to the general store where he would buy a small bag of hard sugar candy, and they would sit on the bench in front of the store, eat their candy and talk. The old people of the village as well as those who rode in from distant ranches knew Rafael was courting her, and knew it was good for both of them. The men tipped their hats as they passed by because Rafael was now a man.

Love grew between the young woman and Rafael. One day she said, "You need someone to take care of you. I will go with you." Her voice filled his heart with joy. They talked to the priest, and he married them, and after Mass there was a feast. The women set up tables in front of the church, covering them with their brightest table oil cloths, and they brought food which they served to everyone who had come to the celebration. The men drank whiskey and talked about the good grass growing high on the llano, and about the herds which would grow and multiply. One of the old men of the village brought out his violin, followed by his friend with his accordion. The two men played the old polkas and the varsilonas while the people danced on the hard-packed dirt in front of the church. The fiesta brought the people of the big and lonely llano together.

The violin and accordion music was accompanied by the clapping of hands and the stamping of feet. The dancing was lively and the people were happy. They laughed and congratulated the young couple. They brought gifts, kitchen utensils for the young bride, ranch tools for Rafael, whiskey for everyone who would drink, real whiskey bought in the general store, not the mula some of the men made in their stills. Even Rafael took a drink, his first drink with the men, and he grew flushed and happy with it. He danced every dance with his young wife and everyone could see that his love was deep and devoted. He laughed with the men when they slapped his back and whispered advice for the wedding night. Then the wind began to rise and it started to rain; the first huge drops mixed with the blowing dust. People sought cover, others hitched their wagons and headed home, all calling their goodbyes and buena suerte in the gathering wind. And so Rafael lifted his young bride onto his horse and they waved goodbye to the remaining villagers as they, too, rode away, south, deep into the empty llano, deep into the storm which came rumbling across the sky with thunder and lightning flashes, pushing the cool wind before it.

And that is how the immense silence of the land and the heavy burden of loneliness came to be lifted from Rafael's heart. His young bride had come to share his life and give it meaning and form. Sometimes late at night when the owl called from its perch on the windmill and the coyotes sang in the hills, he would lie awake and feel the presence of her young, thin body next to his. On such nights the stillness of the spring air and her fragrance intoxicated him and made him

drunk with happiness; then he would feel compelled to rise and walk out into the night which
was bright with the moon and the million stars
which swirled overhead in the sky. He breathed
the cool air of the llano night, and it was like a
liquor which made his head swirl and his heart
pound. He was a happy man.

In the morning she arose before him and
fixed his coffee and brought it to him, and at first
he insisted that it was he who should get up to
start the fire in the wood stove because he was
used to rising long before the sun and riding in
the range while the dawn was alive with its bright
colors, but she laughed and told him she would
spoil him in the summer and in the winter, when
it was cold, he would be the one to rise and start
the fire and bring her coffee in bed. They laughed
and talked during those still-dark, early hours of
the morning. He told her where he would ride
that day and about the work that needed to be
done. She, in turn, told him about the curtains
she was sewing and the cabinet she was painting
and how she would cover each drawer with oil
cloth.

He had whitewashed the inside of the small
adobe home for her, then plastered the outside
walls with mud to keep out the dust which came
with the spring winds and the cold which would
come with winter. He fixed the roof and patched
the leaks, and one night when it rained they
didn't have to rise to catch the leaking water in
pots and pans. They laughed and were happy.
Just as the spring rains made the land green, so
his love made her grow, and one morning she
quietly whispered in his ear that by Christmas
they would have a child.

Her words brought great joy to him. "A child," she had said, and excitement tightened in his throat. That day he didn't work on the range. He had promised her a garden, so he hitched up one of the old horses to his father's plow and he spent all day plowing the soft, sandy earth by the windmill. He spread manure from the corral on the soil and turned it into the earth. He fixed an old pipe leading to the windmill and showed her how to turn it to water the garden. She was pleased. She spent days planting flowers and vegetables. She watered the old, gnarled peach trees near the garden and they burst into a late bloom. She worked the earth with care and by midsummer she was already picking green vegetables to cook with the meat and potatoes. It became a part of his life to stop on the rise above the ranch when he rode in from the range, to pause and watch her working in the garden in the cool of the afternoon. There was something in that image, something which made a mark of permanence on the otherwise empty llano.

Her slender body began to grow heavier. Sometimes he heard her singing, and he knew it was not only to herself she sang or hummed. Sometimes he glanced at her when her gaze was fixed on some distant object, and he realized it was not a distant mesa or cloud she was seeing, but a distant future which was growing in her.

Time flowed past them. He thinned his herds, prepared for the approaching winter, and she gathered the last of the fruits and vegetables. But something was not right. Her excitement of the summer was gone. She began to grow pale and weak. She would rise in the mornings and fix breakfast, then she would have to return to bed and rest. By late December, as the first clouds of winter appeared and the winds from the west blew sharp and cold, she could no longer rise in the mornings. He tried to help, but there was little he could do except sit by her side and keep her silent company while she slept her troubled sleep. A few weeks later a small flow of blood began, as pains and cramps wracked her body. Something was pulling at the child she carried, but it was not the natural rhythm she had expected.

"Go for Doña Rufina," she said, "Go for help!"

He hitched the wagon and made the long drive into the village, arriving at the break of light to rouse the old partera from her sleep. For many years the old woman had delivered the babies born in the village or in the nearby ranches, and now, as he explained what had happened and the need to hurry, she nodded solemnly. She packed the things she would need, then kneeled at her altar and made the sign of the cross. She prayed to el Santo Niño for help and whispered to the Virgin Mary that she would return when her work was done. Then she turned the small statues to face the wall. Rafael helped her on the wagon, loaded her bags, then used the reins as a whip to drive the horses at a fast trot on their long journey back. They arrived at the ranch as the sun was setting. That night a child was born, a girl, pulled from the womb by the old woman's practiced hands. The old woman placed her mouth to the baby's and pushed in air. The baby gasped, sucked in air and came alive. Doña Rufina smiled as she cleaned the small, squirming body. The sound was good. The cry filled the night, shattering the silence in the room.

"A daughter," the old woman said. "A hard birth." She cleaned away the sheets, made the bed, washed the young wife who lay so pale and quiet on the bed, and when there was nothing more she could do she rolled a cigarette and sat back to smoke and wait. The baby lay quietly at her mother's side, while the breathing of the young mother grew weaker and weaker and the blood which the old woman was powerless to stop continued to flow. By morning she was dead. She had opened her eyes and looked at the small white bundle which lay at her side. She smiled and tried to speak, but there was no strength left. She sighed and closed her eyes.

"She is dead," Doña Rufina said.

"No, no," Rafael moaned. He held his wife in his arms and shook his head in disbelief. "She cannot die, she cannot die," he whispered over and over. Her body, once so warm and full of joy, was now cold and lifeless, and he cursed the forces he didn't understand but which had drawn her into that eternal silence. He would never again hear her voice, never hear her singing in her garden, never see her waving as he came over the rise from the llano. A long time later he allowed Doña Rufina's hands to draw him away. Slowly he took the shovel she handed him and dug the grave beneath the peach trees by the garden, that place of shade she had loved so much in the summer and which now appeared so deserted in the December cold. He buried her, then quickly saddled his horse and rode into the llano. He was gone for days. When he returned, he was pale and haggard from the great emptiness which filled him. Doña Rufina was there, caring for the child, nursing her as best she could with the little milk she could draw from the milk cow they kept in the corral. Although the baby was thin and sick with colic, she was alive. Rafael looked only once at the child, then he turned his back to her. In his mind the child had taken the life of his wife, and he didn't care if the baby lived or died. He didn't care if he lived or died. The joy he had known was gone, her soul had been pulled into the silence he felt around him, and his only wish was to be with her. She was out there somewhere, alone and lost on the cold and desolate plain. If he could only hear her voice he was sure he could find her. That was his only thought as he rode out every day across the plain. He rode and listened for her voice in the wind which moaned across the cold landscape, but there was no sound, only the silence. His tortured body was always cold and shivering from the snow and wind, and when the dim sun sank in the west it was his horse which trembled and turned homeward, not he. He would have been content to ride forever, to ride until the cold numbed his body and he could join her in the silence.

When he returned late in the evenings he would eat alone and in silence. He did not speak to the old woman who sat huddled near the stove, holding the baby on her lap, rocking softly back and forth and singing wisps of the old songs. The baby listened, as if she, too, already realized the strangeness of the silent world she had entered. Over them the storms of winter howled and tore at the small home where the three waited for spring in silence. But there was no promise in the spring. When the days grew longer and the earth began to thaw, Rafael threw himself into his work. He separated his herd, branded the new

calves, then drove a few yearlings into the village
where he sold them for the provisions he needed.
But even the silence of the llano carries whispers.
People asked about the child and Doña Rufina,
and only once did he look at them and say, "My
wife is dead." Then he turned away and spoke no
more. The people understood his silence and his
need to live in it, alone. No more questions were
ever asked. He came into the village only when
the need for more provisions brought him, moving like a ghost, a haunted man, a man the silence
of the llano had conquered and claimed. The old
people of the village crossed their foreheads and
whispered silent prayers when he rode by.

Seven years passed, unheeded in time, un-
marked time, change felt only because the seasons changed. Doña Rufina died. During those
years she and Rafael had not exchanged a dozen
words. She had done what she could for the
child, and she had come to love her as her own.
Leaving the child behind was the only regret she
felt the day she looked out the window and heard
the creaking sound in the silence of the day. In
the distance, as if in a whirlwind which swirled
slowly across the llano, she saw the figure of
death riding a creaking cart which moved slowly
towards the ranch house. So, she thought, my co-
madre la muerte comes for me. It is time to leave
this earth. She fed the child and put her to bed,
then she wrapped herself in a warm quilt and sat
by the stove, smoking her last cigarette, quietly
rocking back and forth, listening to the creaking
of the rocking chair, listening to the moan of the
wind which swept across the land. She felt at
peace. The chills she had felt the past month left
her. She felt light and airy, as if she were enter-

ing a pleasant dream. She heard the voices of old
friends she had known on the llano, and she saw
the faces of the many babies she had delivered
during her lifetime. Then she heard a knock on
the door. Rafael, who sat at his bed repairing his
bridle and oiling the leather, heard her say,
"Enter," but he did not look up. He did not hear
her last gasp for air. He did not see the dark figure of the old woman who stood at the door,
beckoning to Doña Rufina.

When Rafael looked up he saw her head slump
forward. He arose and filled a glass with water.
He held her head up and touched the water to
her lips, but it was no use. He knew she was
dead. The wind had forced the door open and it
banged against the wall, filling the room with a
cold gust, awakening the child who started from
her bed. He moved quickly to shut the door, and
the room again became dark and silent. One
more death, one more burial, and again he returned to his work. Only out there, in the vast
space of the llano, could he find something in
which he could lose himself.

Only the weather and the seasons marked
time for Rafael as he watched over his land and
his herd. Summer nights he slept outside, and
the galaxies swirling overhead reminded him he
was alone. Out there, in that strange darkness,
the soul of his wife rested. In the day, when the
wind shifted direction, he sometimes thought he
heard the whisper of her voice. Other times he
thought he saw the outline of her face in the huge
clouds which billowed up in the summer. And always he had to drive away the dream and put away
the voice or the image, because the memory only
increased his sadness. He learned to live alone,

completely alone. The seasons changed, the rains
came in July and the llano was green, then the
summer sun burned it dry. Later the cold of winter came with its fury. And all these seasons he
survived, moving across the desolate land,
hunched over his horse. He was a man who could
not allow himself to dream. He rode alone.

II

And the daughter? What of the daughter?
The seasons brought growth to her, and she grew
into young womanhood. She learned to watch the
man who came and went and did not speak, and
so she, too, learned to live in her own world. She
learned to prepare the food and to sit aside in silence while he ate, to sweep the floor and keep
the small house clean, to keep alive the fire in the
iron stove, and to wash the clothes with the
scrub-board at the water tank by the windmill. In
the summer her greatest pleasure was the cool
place by the windmill where the water flowed.

The year she was sixteen, during springtime
she stood and bathed in the cool water which
came clean and cold out of the pipe, and as she
stood under the water the numbing sensation reminded her of the first time the blood had come.
She had not known what it was: it came without
warning, without her knowledge. She had felt a
fever in the night, and cramps in her stomach,
then in the restlessness of sleep she had awakened and felt the warm flow between her legs.
She was not frightened, but she did remember
that for the first time she became aware of her fa-

ther snoring in his sleep on the bed at the other side of the room. She arose quietly, without disturbing him, and walked out into the summer night, going to the watertank where she washed herself. The water which washed her blood splashed and ran into the garden.

That same summer she felt her breasts mature, her hips widen, and when she ran to gather her chickens into the coop for the night she felt a difference in her movement. She did not think or dwell on it, a dark part of her intuition told her that this was a natural element which belonged to the greater mystery of birth which she had seen take place on the llano around her. She had seen her hens seek secret nests to hatch their eggs, and she knew the proud, clucking noises the hens made when they appeared with the small yellow chicks trailing. There was life in the eggs. Once when the herd was being moved and they came to the water tank to drink she had seen the great bull mount one of the cows, and she remembered the whirling of dust and the bellowing which filled the air. Later, the cow would seek a nest and there would be a calf. These things she knew.

Now she was a young woman. When she went to the watertank to bathe she sometimes paused and looked at her reflection in the water. Her face was smooth and oval, dark from the summer sun, as beautiful as the mother she had not known. When she slipped off her blouse and saw how full and firm her breasts had grown and how rosy the nipples appeared, she smiled and touched them and felt a pleasure she couldn't explain. There had been no one to ask about the changes which came into her life. Once a woman and her daughters had come. She saw the wagon coming up on the road, but instead of going out to greet them she ran and hid in the house, watching through parted curtains as the woman and her daughters came and knocked at the door. She could hear them calling in strange words, words she did not know. She huddled in the corner and kept very still until the knocking at the door had ceased, then she edged closer to the window and watched as they climbed back on the wagon, laughing and talking in a strange, exciting way. Long after they were gone she could still smell the foreign, sweet odors they had brought to her doorstep.

After that, no one came. She remembered the words of Doña Rufina and often spoke them aloud just to hear the sound they made as they exploded from her lips. "Lumbre," she said in the morning when she put kindling on the banked ashes in the stove, whispering the word so the man who slept would not hear her. "Agua," she said when she drew water at the well. "Viento de diablo," she hissed to let her chickens know a swirling dust storm was on its way, and when they did not respond she reverted to the language she had learned from them and with a clucking sound she drove them where she wanted. "Tote! Tote!" she called and made the clicking sound for danger when she saw the gray figure of the coyote stalking close to the ranch house. The chickens understood and hurried into the safety of the coop. She learned to imitate the call of the wild doves. In the evening when they came to drink at the water tank she called to them, and they sang back. The roadrunner which came to chase lizards near the windmill learned to "cou" for her, and the wild sparrows and other birds also heard her call and grew to know her presence. They fed at her feet like chickens.

When the milk cow wandered away from the corral she learned to whistle to bring it back. She invented other sounds, other words, words for the seasons and the weather they brought, words for the birds she loved, words for the juniper and piñon and yucca and wild grass which grew on the llano, words for the light of the sun and dark of the night, words which when uttered broke the silence of the long days she spent alone, never words to be shared with the man who came to eat late in the evenings, who came enveloped in silence, his eyes cast down in a bitterness she did not understand. He ate the meals she served in silence, then he smoked a cigarette, then he slept. Their lives were unencumbered by each other's presence, they did not exist for each other, each had learned to live in a silent world.

But other presences began to appear on the llano, even at this isolated edge of the plain which lay so far beyond the village of Las Animas. Men came during the season of the yellow moon, and they carried long sticks which made thunder. In that season when the antelope were rutting they came, and she could hear the sound of the thunder they made, even feel the panic of the antelopes which ran across the llano. "Hunters!" her father said, and he spat the word like a curse. He did not want them to enter his world, but still they came, not in the silent, horse-drawn wagons, but in an iron wagon which made noise and smoked.

The sound of these men frightened her. Life on the llano grew tense as they drew near. One

day, five of the hunters drove up to the ranch
house in one of their iron wagons. She moved
quickly to lock the door, to hide, for she had seen
the antelope they had killed hung over the front
of their wagon, a beautiful tan-colored buck splat-
tered with blood. It was tied with rope and wire,
its dry tongue hanging from its mouth, its large
eyes still open. The men pounded on the door
and called her father's name. She held her breath
and peered through the window. She saw them
drink from a bottle they passed to each other.
They pounded on the door again and fired their
rifles into the air, filling the llano with explosions.
The smell of burned powder filled the air. The
house seemed to shake as they called words she
did not understand. "Rafael!" they called. "A virgin daughter!" They roared with laughter as they
climbed in their wagon, and the motor shrieked
and roared as they drove away. All day the vibration of the noise and awful presence of the men
lay over the house, and at night in nightmares she
saw the faces of the men, heard their laughter
and the sound of the rifle's penetrating roar as it
shattered the silence of the llano. Two of them
had been young men, broad-shouldered boys who
looked at the buck they had killed and smiled.
The faces of these strange men drifted through
her dreams and she was at once afraid and attracted by them.

One night in her dreams she saw the face of
the man who lived there, the man Doña Rufina
had told her was to be called father, and she
could not understand why he should appear in
her dream. When she awoke she heard the owl
cry a warning from its perch on the windmill. She
hurried outside, saw the dark form of the coyote

slinking toward the chicken coop. A snarl hissed in her throat as she threw a rock, and instantly the coyote faded into the night. She waited in the dark, troubled by her dream and by the appearance of the coyote, then she slipped quietly back into the house. She did not want to awaken the man, but he was awake. He, too, had heard the coyote, and had heard her slip out, but he said nothing. In the warm summer night, each lay awake, encased in their solitary silence, expecting no words, but aware of each other as animals are aware when another is close by, as she had been aware even in her sleep that the coyote was drawing near.

III

One afternoon Rafael returned home early. He had seen a cloud of dust on the road to his ranch house. It was not the movement of cattle, and it wasn't the dust of the summer dustdevils. The rising dust could only mean there was a car on the road. He cursed under his breath, remembering the signs he had posted on his fence, and the chain with a lock he had bought in the village to secure his gate. He did not want to be bothered, he would keep everyone away. For a time he continued to repair the fence, using his horse to draw the wire taut, nailing the barbed wire to the cedar posts he had set that morning. The day was warm, he sweated as he worked, but again he paused. Something made him restless, uneasy. He wiped his brow and looked towards the ranch house. Perhaps it was only his imagination, he thought, perhaps the whirlwind was only a mir-

age, a reflection of the strange uneasiness he felt.
He looked to the west where two buzzards circled
over the coyote he had shot that morning. Soon
they would drop to feed. Around him the ants
scurried through the dry grass, working their
hills as he worked his land. There was the buzz of
grasshoppers, the occasional call of prairie dogs,
each sound in its turn absorbed into the hum
which was the silence of the land. He continued
his work but the image of the cloud of dust returned, the thought of strangers on his land filled
him with anger and apprehension. The bad feeling grew until he couldn't work. He packed his
tools, swung on his horse and rode homeward.

Later, as he sat on his horse at the top of the
rise from where he could view his house, the uneasy feeling grew more intense. Something was
wrong, someone had come. Around him a strange
dark cloud gathered, shutting off the sun, stirring
the wind into frenzy. He urged his horse down
the slope and rode up to the front door. All was
quiet. The girl usually came out to take his horse
to the corral where she unsaddled and fed it, but
today there was no sight of her. He turned and
looked towards the windmill and the plot of
ground where he had buried his wife. The pile of
rocks which marked her grave was almost covered by wind-swept sand. The peach trees were
almost dead. The girl had watered them from
time to time, as she had watered the garden, but
no one had helped or taught her and so her ef-
forts were poorly rewarded. Only a few flowers
survived in the garden, spots of color in the otherwise dry, tawny landscape.

His horse moved uneasily beneath him; he
dismounted slowly. The door of the house was

ajar, he pushed it open and entered. The room was dark and cool, the curtains at the window were drawn, the fire for the evening meal was not yet started. Outside, the first drops of rain fell on the tin roof as the cloud darkened the land. In the room, a fly buzzed. Perhaps the girl is not here, he thought, maybe it is just that I am tired and I have come early to rest. He turned toward the bed and saw her. She sat huddled on the bed, her knees drawn up, her arms wrapped around them. She looked at him, her eyes terrified and wild in the dim light. He started to turn away but he heard her make a sound, the soft cry of an injured animal.

"Rafael!" she moaned as she reached out for him. "Rafael ...."

He felt his knees grow weak. She had never used his name before.

At the same time she flung back the crumpled sheet and pointed to the stain of blood. He shook his head, gasped. Her blouse was torn off, red scratch marks scarred her white shoulders, tears glistened in her eyes as she reached out again and whispered his name. "Rafael .... Rafael ...."

Someone had come in that cloud of dust, perhaps a stray vaquero looking for work, perhaps one of the men from the village who knew she was here alone, a man had come in the whirlwind and forced himself into the house. "Oh, God ...." he groaned as he stepped back, felt the door behind him, saw her rise from the bed, her arms outstretched, the curves of her breasts rising and falling as she gasped for breath and called his name, "Rafael .... Rafael ...." She held out her arms, and he heard his scream echo in the small adobe room which had suddenly become a prison suffocating him. Still the girl came towards him, her eyes dark and piercing, her dark hair falling over her shoulders and throat. With great effort, he found the strength to turn and flee. Outside, he grabbed the reins of his frightened horse, mounted and dug his spurs into the sides of the poor creature. Whipping it hard he rode away from the ranch and what he had seen.

Once before he had fled, on the day he buried his wife. He had seen her face then, as he now saw the image of the girl, saw her eyes burning into him, saw the torn blouse, the bed, and most frightening of all, heard her call his name, "Rafael .... Rafael ...." It opened and broke the shell of his silence. It was a wound which brought back the ghost of his wife, the beauty of her features which he now saw again and which blurred into the image of the girl. He spurred the horse until it buckled with fatigue and sent him crashing into the earth. The impact brought a searing pain and the peace of darkness.

He didn't know how long he lay unconscious. When he awoke he touched his throbbing forehead and felt the clotted blood. The pain in his head was intense, but he could walk. Without direction he stumbled across the llano only to find that late in the afternoon when he looked around he saw his ranch house. He approached the water tank to wash the dried blood from his face, then he stumbled into the tool shed by the corral and tried to sleep. Dusk came, the bats and night hawks flew over the quiet llano, night fell and still he could not sleep. Through the chinks of the weathered boards he could see the house and the light which burned at the window. The girl was awake. All night he stared at the light burning at the window, and in his fever he saw her face again, her pleading eyes, the curve of her young breasts, her arms as she reached up and called his name. Why had she called his name? Why? Was it the devil who rode the whirlwind? Was it the devil who had come to break the silence of the llano? He groaned and shivered as the call of the owl sounded in the night. He looked into the darkness and thought he saw the figure of the girl walking to the water tank. She bathed her shoulders in the cold water, bathed her body in the moonlight. Then the owl grew still and the figure in the flowing gown disappeared as the first sign of dawn appeared in the clouds of the east.

He rose and entered the house, tremulously, unsure of what he would find. There was food on the table and hot coffee on the stove. She had prepared his breakfast as she had all those years, and now she sat by the window, withdrawn, her face pale and thin. She looked up at him, but he turned away and sat at the table with his back to her. He tried to eat but the food choked him. He drank the strong coffee, then he rose and hurried outside. He cursed as he reeled towards the corral like a drunken man, then he stopped suddenly and shuddered with a fear he had never known before. He shook his head in disbelief and raised his hand as if to ward away the figure sitting at the huge cedar block at the woodpile. It was the figure of a woman, a woman who called his name and beckoned him. And for the first time in sixteen years he called out his wife's name.

"Rita," he whispered. "Rita ...."

Yes, it was she, he thought, sitting there as she used to, laughing and teasing while he chopped firewood. He could see her eyes, her smile, hear her voice. He remembered how he would show off his strength with the axe, and she would compliment him in a teasing way as she gathered the chips of piñon and cedar for kindling. "Rita ...." he whispered, and moved toward her, but now the figure sitting at the woodblock was the girl, she sat there, calling his name, smiling and coaxing him as a demon of hell would entice the sinner into the center of the whirlwind. "No!" he screamed and grabbed the axe. Lifting it, he brought it down on the dark heart of the swirling vortex. The blow split the block in half and splintered the axe handle. He felt the pain of the vibration numb his arms. The devil is dead, he thought, opened his eyes, saw only the split block and the splintered axe in front of him. He shook his head and backed away, crying to God to exorcize the possession in his tormented soul. And even as he prayed for respite he looked up and saw the window. Behind the parted curtains he saw her face, his wife, the girl, the pale face of the woman who haunted him.

Without saddling the horse he mounted and spurred it south. He had to leave this place, he would ride south until he could ride no more, until he disappeared into the desert. He would ride into oblivion, and when he was dead the tightness and pain in his chest and the torturous thoughts would be gone, then there would be peace. He would die and give himself to the silence, and in that element he would find rest. But, without warning, a dark whirlwind rose before him, and in the midst of the storm he saw a woman. She did not smile, she did not call his name, her horse was the dark clouds which towered over him, the cracking of her whip a fire which filled the sky. Her laughter rumbled across the sky and shook the earth, her shadow swirled around him, blocking out the sun, filling the air with choking dust, driving fear into both man and animal until they turned in a wide circle back towards the ranch house. And when he found himself once again on the small rise by his home, the whirlwind lifted and the woman disappeared. The thunder rumbled in the distance, then was gone. The air grew quiet around him. He could hear himself breathe, he could hear the pounding of his heart. Around him the sun was bright and warm.

He didn't know how long he sat there remembering other times when he had paused at that place to look down at his home. He was startled from his reverie by the slamming of a screen door. He looked and saw the girl walk towards the water tank. He watched her as she pulled the pipe clear of the tank, then she removed her dress and began to bathe. Her white skin glistened in the sunlight as the spray of water splashed over her body. Her long black hair fell over her shoulders to her waist, glistening from the water. He could hear her humming. He remembered his wife bathing there, covering herself with soap foam, and he remembered how he would sit and smoke while she bathed, and his life was full of peace and contentment. She would wrap a towel around her body and come running to sit by his side in the sun, and as she dried her hair they would talk. Her words had filled the silence of that summer. Her words were an extension of the love she had brought him.

And now? He touched his legs to the horse's sides and the horse moved, making its way down the slope towards the water tank. She turned, saw him coming, and she stepped out of the stream of the cascading water to gather a towel around her naked body. She waited quietly. He rode up to her, looked at her, looked for a long time at her face and into her eyes. Then slowly he dismounted and walked to her. She waited in silence. He moved towards her, and with a trembling hand he reached out and touched her wet hair.

"Rita," he said. "Your name is Rita."

She smiled at the sound. She remembered the name from long ago. It was a sound she remembered from Doña Rufina. It was the sound the axe made when it rang against hard cedar wood, and now, he, the man who had lived in silence all those years, he had spoken the name.

It was a good sound which brought joy to her heart. This man had come to speak this sound which she remembered. She saw him turn and point at the peach trees at the edge of the garden.

"Your mother is buried over there," he said. "This was her garden. The spring is the time for the garden. I will turn the earth for you. The seeds will grow."

❖

"My father was a gentle man," she tells me, "a real caballero. All the people loved him. Oh, some day you will know the truth, my little one. He was a man of honor, a proud man. He rode so tall and noble. The women of Platero pretended to sweep their doorsteps when he rode by, but they really came out to admire him. And he would smile and tip his sombrero, then he would ride home to me. I was his jewel, his angel, his only daughter...."

THE
ROAD
TO
PLATERO

Everyone in the village knows that a ghost rides the road to Platero. Everyone watches, everyone waits, and at night we can hear the hoofbeats of the caballero's horse as he rides on that lonely road. During the long, hot days my mother sings sad lullabies while she sits by the window and stares down the deserted road. She sighs when she sings, and she holds me on her lap and draws me close. I can feel the gentle pounding of her heart when she tells me that the caballero who haunts the road to Platero is the ghost of her father.

"Oh, he was a handsome man," she sings to me and tells me stories of the past, tales of her youth, times when Platero was the most thriving and beautiful village on the entire llano. "Then death came," she sighs. "Love came, death came, then you were born, my little son ...."

31

The wind dies at dusk. My mother's hands dart like nervous birds as she moves around the kitchen, touching things absentmindedly. Her breath quickens, and from time to time she stops to listen. The vaqueros of Platero are returning from the llano. In the distance we can hear the thunder of their hot and tired horses. The other women of the village go to their windows and look out into the desolate llano. They know their men are coming, hungry from a long day's work, riding hard so they will not see the ghost horseman who haunts the road.

My father rides with the vaqueros. For him the road is haunted, and every day I hear him curse God and torment his horse with whip and spur. He must drink for courage to ride that stretch of road where, my mother says, he killed her father.

Once, my mother tells me, it was a well-traveled road and everyone came to her father's ranch. There were good times and fiestas for every occasion. Now, only these wild and brawling men-creatures ride the road to Platero.

"My father was a gentle man," she tells me, "a real caballero. All the people loved him. Oh, some day you will know the truth, my little one. He was a man of honor, a proud man. He rode so tall and noble. The women of Platero pretended to sweep their doorsteps when he rode by, but they really came out to admire him. And he would smile and tip his sombrero, then he would ride home to me. I was his jewel, his angel, his only daughter ...."

She tells me stories I have heard many times before, and I see how the memories make her heart pound. Purple veins rise on her temples, and I can almost see the images of violence and love which stir in her blood. Sometimes terrible dreams trouble my sleep, and I, too, am filled with fear.

"This man, this beast destroyed the dreams of my father!" she cries, and her anguish and fury make my blood run cold. I see her reach for the knife on the table. She raises it high. "I will keep this near my heart, my father, and I will do your will. There is no pride nor honor left in Platero, father." Then she turns to me and whispers, "I have submitted to that beast only to protect you, my son, but you are a man like any other man. Will you, too, raise your spurs and rake your mother's flanks when you are grown?" She laughs bitterly. "Yes, we are the slaves of our fathers, our husbands, our sons ... and you, my little one, my life, you will grow to be a man ...."

The vaqueros of Platero arrive like a whirlwind. In the corral the mares paw the ground nervously as the stallions enter. The men laugh and call out, then there is silence. We wait, his footsteps sound on the porch, his spurs jingle, my mother makes the sign of the cross on her forehead. Her eyes stare with cold determination, then a strange smile curls her lips. "I loved him once," she whispers, and her trembling hands hide the knife. He enters and stands looking at her. He only looks at me to curse me. Then he sits, unbuckles his spurs, raises them and runs them slowly across his stubbled cheek.

"What evil have you been up to, my Carmelita," he grins and taunts her. "What lies have you been telling your son?"

"I tell him of the man who rides a red stallion to Platero," she answers calmly.

He stands and shouts. "It is not a man! It is a devil!"

"He will return to Platero," she insists. I crawl into a corner where I watch and make no noise. I am afraid of his wrath, and now I fear her will.

"You evil woman," he accuses. "Can you tell him the truth? I will tell him who mounted his mother!"

"No!" she cries. "No! He is innocent. He knows nothing. Can't we forget the past ....?" She beckons him with her lovely hands. Of all the women in Platero, my mother is the youngest. She is thin, her hair is long and black, her skin is smooth. From the porch I have seen the vaqueros admire the sleek, beautiful mares, and I have seen them look at my mother.

He laughs and picks up his bottle. "So you want to play the game," he sneers. "Come and pull off my boots."

My mother hurries to help him with his boots. Outside, the stallions circle the mares, I hear them cry in the corral.

The moon hangs pallid in the dark sky. It bathes the black mesa, shadows move like witches. My mother rises, sweat covers her body. She shivers as she parts the curtains and looks into the darkness. In the small adobe homes around us other women also rise from their labors and peer into the night. They watch the pale moonlight cast its spell while their men sleep. My mother comes to me and covers me with a quilt. She holds me and we listen in silence for the sound of the caballero who rides toward Platero.

"Father," my mother whispers. "I swear to you, you will have your peace and rest. I will avenge ...."

In the morning the vaqueros leave. It has been this way since I can remember. It is cool inside our adobe home before the strong sun comes to bake the land. My mother sweeps the floor, beads of perspiration wet her face. She hums a lullaby for me while she works. She opens the door to let in the cool morning breeze. "To air our home of the evil of the night," she says. She gazes at the houses scattered along the dusty road and yearns to visit with the other women, but she cannot. They know the secret she keeps from me. They nod in greeting, that is all, and watch her in silence. Only one woman does not work. She sits by her door in the shade of a purple plumed tamarisk and smokes cigarettes. She laughs softly when she sees my mother.

In the afternoon the wind rises, whipping the whirlwinds across the bare earth. My mother says they are the work of the devil. Sometimes huge sandstorms envelop the land, our house shudders, the day turns into night. Then my mother holds me close and whispers many things, but never the secret which causes so much anguish in her heart.

Every day the women wait in the oppressive heat, waiting for their men to return. Sometimes I see the faces of other children at the dark windows, pale, drawn faces, and sad eyes which seem to bear the curse which revolves around me and my mother. There is no hope in Platero, there is only the waiting for the vaqueros as they come stinging their horses with their cruel whips and spurring blood from their soft flanks.

I know my father is coming long before my mother whispers to me. She moves nervously, the cup she is holding falls and shatters on the

floor. She stoops and gathers the broken pieces.
"Fragments of the past," she murmurs as she
stares at them. She sobs gently. The cup was a
gift from her father, and every year on her
birthday he would take it from the cupboard, fill it
with wine and drink to her health and beauty. He
was never displeased that he had no sons, his
dream was that she would be a great lady, the
woman who would inherit all the lands of Platero.

"He thought time was his ally and he would
live forever," she cries, "but he was wrong. Now
there is only you, my son."

She dries her eyes with her apron and moves
to the window to look into the gathering, somber
dusk. "The nighthawks are flying low," she says,
"so it will rain tonight." The ground reverberates
with hoofbeats. We hear shouts and the sharp
crack of whips, then the whistle of the vaqueros
as they unsaddle their horses and turn them loose
in the corral. My mother shudders, and I know
her resolution wavers when she catches sight of
him.

On the portal I hear his sharp spurs jingle,
then the door opens and he fills the house like a
howling wind, his harsh laughter echoes in the
room.

"Ah, my Carmelita," he says, "have you been
doing penance for your sins?"

My mother lights the farol; in its light the
shadows rise and move like ghosts. Outside the
dark rumbles with the approaching storm. My father eats and drinks while we wait, and when he
is done he grabs her arm as she passes. He pulls
her into the room beyond the kitchen and I hear
her cries and groans. I turn to see the lightning
flash at the window, the rain falls in torrents, and

I feel the ominous dread which fills the night.

"There is still time," I hear her say. "Forgiveness will wash away all these years of torture, the ghost which haunts you ...."

His laughter is as savage as the thunder.

"We can forget the past," she prays, and I know that she has closed her eyes to imagine him as she saw him the first time he rode into the village.

"No, my Carmelita," he says with hate in his voice. "Your father made sure that we could never forget the past ...."

"Forgive," my mother pleads.

"Forgive? Oh, no, your sin is too dark to be forgiven," he taunts her. "Your sin is the sin of hell, and you will do penance by serving me forever. Only your penance can keep away that devil which rides the road at night."

He goes to the window to smoke and drink. The lightning flashes and I see his face. For the first time I see that he is afraid of the ghostly caballero who nightly circles Platero. He curses the coyotes that cry fearfully in the hills, calling them witches of the devil. In her bed my mother rocks back and forth, her vacant eyes stare into the past. She knows what she must do.

When he is finished drinking he throws the bottle aside and goes to stand over her. He is never done with his tormenting. He twists his hand into her hair and pulls her to her feet.

"I killed your father for this worthless land!" he shouts. "But I made the mistake of not killing him sooner." He looks at me, then savagely flings her across the room. "Whore!" he spits, then opens the door and moves into the night. "Ghost of Platero!" he shouts at the darkness. "Take your daughter!" He laughs. We hear him laughing as he goes to the woman of the tamarisk tree.

The storm has passed. Now only gentle drops of rain drum on the roof. My mother wraps a blanket around her shoulders and clasps me in her arms. "Platero is hell, my little one," she says as we go to the window. The night is silver with moonlight. Somewhere a woman laughs in the dark. I lie quietly and try to sleep, but not even her gentle caress can keep away the monsters which ride into my dreams.

"Sleep, my little angel," she sings, "my father returns to avenge us ...." And she sings of the caballero who was her father, he who rode proud and tall on a red stallion.

Late in the night my father returns, his face ashen with fear.

"I saw him," he cries, "I swear I saw him! Always before it was only a shadow, but tonight I saw him!"

"He is dead," my mother moans.

"Damn you! You were not worth the killing!" he curses.

She screams as if in pain. "Oh, let me rest! Torment me no more!"

"He is out there!" my father shouts as he glances out the window, a ring of fear in his voice. "He haunts the road!"

"He comes to avenge us," my mother says coldly. I see her hands clutch the dagger near her heart.

"Let him come," my father cries, "I killed him once, I will kill him again."

"Murderer!" my mother screams, and instantly he is on her, striking hard, sending her crashing to the floor. He unwinds his whip and cracks it over her.

"Whore! Witch!!" he fouls the air with his curses. "It is you whose sin brings the ghost of hell to our doorstep. You will be happy with that devil! Come! Go with him!"

He grabs her hair and jerks her to her feet. "Go!" He laughs as he pushes her across the room to the door. Outside the door, the horseman has arrived.

My mother smiles, her eyes light up. "He has come," she cries and without hesitation she takes the dagger and strikes. My father gasps as the steel cuts through his chest, a look of terror contorts his face.

"Now for you, my son!" my mother exclaims and strikes again.

"Witch!" he groans and lifts his sharp spurs and slashes at her. My mother cries out in pain as the spurs cut a deep gash along her throat. Her blood gushes out, mixing with his as he stumbles forward. "Rest in hell!" he hisses and slashes again, and together they fall to the floor, still striking at each other until there is no strength left and their bodies lie still.

It is done, the torment is done .... I feel death enter the room. Strangely, a peace seems to settle over them as they lie in each other's arms. Outside, the wind dies and the streets of the village are quiet. The women of Platero sleep, a restless sleep. In the corral the mares shift uneasily and cry in the dark. The horseman who haunted the road is gone, and only the gentle moonlight shimmers on the road to Platero.

Long ago he used to work the line in front of me; we were friends then. But now he has moved to the front of the long line which relentlessly moves along the river valley. We used to talk when we paused to rest. One day we joked when a bird dropped bird shit on his head. Now he is the leader and we are no longer friends. I wonder how he became the leader. I don't remember, but he must have performed an extraordinary feat to allow him to move to the head of our small wandering tribe.

THE PLACE OF THE SWALLOWS

Again our tribe of boys is at the river, stumbling in the dense, green darkness, cutting a trail through the thick undergrowth which engulfs us.

It seems we are always at the river, gathering by the bank before the first rays of the sun have cut away the damp mist, breathing the night air which clings like veils of lace to the spongy earth, moving in a thin line towards the dark recesses which we can never conquer, emerging only at the end of day. We move like shadows in the darkness, struggling to keep up with the leader. "Why?" I ask myself with each swing of the long knife I use to clear the trail.

Behind me I can hear the breathing of the boy who follows me; ahead, I catch only glimpses of a sweating, brown back and the swinging knife which hacks away at the thick brush. The trail can never end if it follows the river, I think.

Startled birds fly up around us and utter fearful cries; the only other sound is the swishing of
the machetes we use — Machetes?　Kitchen
knives stolen from our mothers' kitchens and carried secretly to the camp where in the ritual of
the campfire they become our hunting instru-
ments; or slabs of steel scavenged from the old
man's refuse heap and honed sharp on his grind-
ing stone, the one he keeps for his axes. The fire
in the stone puts an edge on the common steel,
changes what is simple and honest in the light of
day into a weapon that can draw blood. I know
how the tribe uses fire ....

Even now, as we are gathered around the
campfire, the dancing light and shadows play on
our faces and create a circle of changing masks. I
glance at the others, searching for a clue in their
eyes. I want to know how they feel about the day's
adventure. Everyone is relaxed, some are mending their equipment, others sharpening their
knives. I look at the leader and wonder if he will
ask me to tell the story tonight.

I have an uneasy feeling in my stomach. All
day I have known that someone will have to tell
the story of today's exploration; someone will be
chosen to give form to our exploits. It is always
like this. Before we leave the camp for the night
the talk will turn to our adventure, someone will
pick up the thread of our story and tell it. Some
are very good at it, I am not.

I know the moment for telling the story
comes as unexpected as the force of night when
one is not quite ready for it. Suddenly all the
members of the tribe are silent; only the cries of
the birds from the river and the hissing of the fire
can be heard, that and the sound of the wind

moaning across the empty flats. Then everyone
looks at the chosen one, and the silence can be
broken only by the words which begin the story.
The story teller must begin; he can leave nothing
out; he must tell the story of the tribe's wander-
ings, and he must tell the truth.

Tonight their eyes focus on me. I feel their
stares, and the only way I can relieve the tension
is to begin.

I ask to speak in the name of the tribe and
the leader nods. In the flickering light of the fire
I look for a clue on his face. What does he feel
about the day's adventure, what does he want the
tribe to hear, what did he learn at the Place of the
Swallows?

Long ago he used to work the line in front of
me; we were friends then. But now he has moved
to the front of the long line which relentlessly
moves along the river valley. We used to talk
when we paused to rest. One day we joked when
a bird dropped bird shit on his head. Now he is
the leader and we are no longer friends. I wonder how he became the leader. I don't remember, but he must have performed an extraordinary
feat to allow him to move to the head of our small,
wandering tribe. I look at him, and when our
eyes meet another dread fills my heart. Suddenly
I realize that someday I may be the leader. Someday it will be my turn to meet an unknown enemy,
perhaps one of the many shadows that stalk the
river. Then my courage will be tested, and if I am
victorious the tribe will cheer me, raise me on
their shoulders and that night by the campfire I
will be their new leader.

I shiver. As my lungs draw breath to begin
the story, I think of home .... I sense the warmth

of my mother's kitchen and the strong presence
of my father. There is light in our home, and
there is protection from the cold air that comes
swiftly across the flats as soon as the sun sets.
Here there is only the meager light of the small
fire, barely warming my hands and face while the
cold air that creeps up from the river freezes my
back.

I stutter and begin, but I begin the wrong story! I begin the story of the killing of the giant river turtle and I realize that happened in a different
time and at another place along the river. That
story has already been told! I glance at the others
and the look in their eyes makes me tremble. I
curse myself for thinking of that incident tonight.
Why did it suddenly flood my thoughts? Is it because the killer of the river turtle is gone and I
know he is doomed to tell his story wherever he
goes? I look at the empty place in the circle
where he used to sit. I begin again.

"Today," I hear myself say, *"a story was created as we hunted along the river. Our explorations
took us into unknown territory. There are no stories that tell of anyone ever crossing the great
swamp that lies to the south, but today, with the
urging of our leader, we crossed that dangerous
place ...."*

I hear murmurs of approval, then I feel the
leader's nod. The tribe is happy tonight. One boy
has brought tobacco, stolen from his father's
store, I'm sure. Now it is rolled and lighted and
passed around so we can all smoke as the story
unfolds. When it is my turn, I take a deep breath
and fill my lungs with smoke. As I breathe out I
feel dizzy. My muscles relax. I close my eyes and
continue the story, this time at a slower pace and

with more rhythm. I sway to the chant of the
words that come pouring out to tell of the day's
adventure. I grow bolder with my descriptions.

*"Oh, it was a miserable place, thick with
brush which our trusty machetes cut away,
treacherous with quicksand which sucked at our
legs, and crawling with poisonous snakes. Our
brave leader killed one to clear the way for those
of us who came behind."*

Again there are murmurs and nods of approval. I feel the leader smile in the dark. Tomorrow
he may invite me to walk with him, to carry his
machete and to learn how to lead the tribe along
the river. He may want to teach me how to meet
the sudden dangers that lie in wait in the dark ...
but that's not what this story is about.

I am ready to resume when suddenly there is
a signal from our sentry, and the night air is
chilled with the horrifying scream of an animal.
Something is stalking our camp! We grab our
weapons and freeze, ready to move at the next
signal, but after long, breathless moments we
hear the hoot of an owl. All is clear; there is no
cause for alarm. I feel the hackles of my back sub-
side. My sweating hand clutches my soiled weapon. I curse myself and wonder how I dare to
question the leader when I still rely on cold steel.
I toss the knife away and try to relax and return to
the thread of the story. The interruption makes
it clear that there is a special time which the telling of the story creates, a time and place which
become more important than the adventure lived.
Why? I ask myself. What do the words create? In
the story the small marsh becomes a swamp, slipping into mud becomes a near-fatal fall into the
quagmire, and the stoning of a harmless garter

snake becomes the killing of a poisonous viper. In the shadows of the river I make them see giant monsters, unknown enemies which I know are only reflections of the words I use. I choose details carefully and weave them all into the image. They see themselves as heroes and nod their approval.

I laugh and remind them of the exploits of two new members of the tribe. *"They whacked at a hanging vine and cried out that it was a snake,"* I say, *"and when the wind blew in the trees they said they heard monsters!"* Laughter of ridicule floats in the air; the new boys wince; I feel the power of my words. But still I am uneasy. There is something I am wanting to say; I want to get to the germ of the story in today's adventure. The night wears on; I know I must get to it.

"And when we had crossed that dismal swamp, the river valley narrowed into a gorge, and the walls of the canyon were so high and the growth so thick the sun was shut out. There was only dim light to guide us. Surely our courage and our steel were tested in that dark pit. The air was thick with sulfurous gases, and in the dark, strange animals cried for our blood. On one side the raging river rushed past us and one false step would have sent us to our death. But our courage served us well and the instinct of our leader was great. Never wavering, he cut a path for us to follow. When we had finally carved our way out of that stinking and fearful jungle we came upon the place where the river gorge widened — The Place Where the Swallows Died," I add quickly and hear a murmur of dissension. I feel their bodies shift uneasily in the dark.

"In that canyon the river widened into a large,

deep lake, and springs of clear, sweet water flowed from the earth and we drank our fill. In the trees the birds sang sweetly, and berries grew in abundance in that quiet paradise. We found strange writings on the rock cliffs, the signs of another tribe which had visited that shelter long before we found it. The sides of the lake were lined with clean, sparkling sand, and in the waters swam the large golden carp which we caught and ate ...."

I pause and remember that in another story it was forbidden to eat the golden river fish. I am about to remind the tribe of their sin when a grunt from the leader cuts me short. I feel cold sweat wet my body. He does not want the mood of the tribe spoiled, and I have already gone too far.

"After we ate," I continue, *" we went swimming in the lake and then we lay naked on the clean sand. Above us the swallows flew, like dancers, they swirled and darted high above the cliffs of the gorge that imprisoned us. When they fly high there will be no rain, our leader said, and that is good because when the rains flood this canyon there is no escape. We marveled at his wisdom while looking at the high water marks on the sides of the sandstone cliffs, and it was true, when the flash floods came the paradise became a tomb of water. We were thankful that our leader could read the signs, and so we rested peacefully.*

"The swallows darted and danced brilliantly in the clear blue sky while we played on the sandbars of the river. Glistening wet and naked we wrestled with each other, and the leader oversaw our contests, awarding prizes to the winners. When we were tired we sat in the shade of the

*trees and talked. Some talked about women and
the things they knew of women, and others whispered the vague dreams and desires which
thoughts of women brought into their nights.
Overhead, the swallows danced ....*

Suddenly something in the air is not pure.
The fire is dying and the clean scent of green juniper is gone. The story has already lasted too
long, it is missing its mark. The wind shifts and a
new smell curls at my nostrils; it is the smell of
sweat and rotten eggs. In the fading light a gold-
en speck on my arm catches my eyes. I scratch
and lift the flake of yellow, dried egg, encrusted
on my skin like spent semen. I rub the fleck of
egg with my fingers and it crumbles into dust.

It is then that I remember how the leader
called us away from our rest. He pointed to the
cliffs where the mud nests of the swallows clung
like beehives to the bare stone. The nests covered the huge slabs of rock.

*"We have been deceived, our leader cried an-
grily, it is the season of the eggs! It's the male
swallows which fly high! We have been deceived!
He picked up a stone and sent it crashing against
the mud nests. The fragile mud and straw came
falling down and the female swallow darted into
flight, cruelly awakened from her time of waiting."*

The leader clears his throat, as if to stop me,
but I continue, and the uneasiness I have felt all
night leaves me.

*"We were called into battle and we obeyed;
that peaceful gorge became our battleground. Our
missiles found their marks as our barrage of rocks
and sticks rained upon the nests. The startled
cries of the swallows pierced the air, but we were*

without mercy! The dry nests exploded with dust and downy feathers which fell earthward and covered us. The blood of the swallows dripped from the high cliffs, mixed with bits of eggshell and yellow mucous it rained upon our heads and covered us, and still we did not stop until we were too tired to lift our arms! Oh, God, only then did we look around and see what we had done. Some of us went to the river to wash away the stains; I stood and watched the juices of the shattered eggs drain into the once-clean sand. Overhead, the swallows cried ...."

I pause to catch my breath. I feel a tension in the cold night air. The silence erodes my story; there is nothing more to say. The fire licks at the wind and dies. One by one the members of the tribe stand and leave, without looking at me, without saying a word. The leader stands and looks at me for a long time, his icy stare cuts through me, but he cannot hurt me; and when I look at him I know that I spoke the truth and that my power has been greater than his. We both know that I won't be here in the morning, but I don't care, I have made my choice. He turns and leaves, and for a long time I sit alone, staring into the glowing embers. An animal cries in the dark, a gust of wind makes the sparks fly, then all is quiet again. I stand and face the darkness of the river's shadows, and the night through which I must walk alone.

The humid air was tense. Somewhere to my left I heard the river murmur as it swept south, and for the first time the dissatisfaction which had been building within me surfaced. I cursed the oppressive darkness and wished I was free of it. I thought of my father walking in the sunlight of his green fields, and wished I was with him. But it was not so; I owed the tribe my allegiance. Today I would become a full member. I would kill the first animal we encountered.

SALOMON'S

STORY

Before I came here I was a hunter, but that was long ago. Still, it was in the pursuit of the hunt that I came face to face with my destiny. This is my story.

We called ourselves a tribe and we spent our time hunting and fishing along the river. For young boys that was a great adventure. Each morning I stole away from my father's home to meet my fellow hunters by the river. My father was a farmer who planted corn on the hills bordering the river. He was a good man. He kept the ritual of the seasons, marked the path of the sun and the moon across the sky, and he prayed each day that the order of things not be disturbed.

He did his duty and tried to teach me about the rhythm in the weather and the seasons, but a wild urge in my blood drove me from him. I went willingly to join the tribe along the river. The call

55

of the hunt was exciting, and daily the slaughter of the animals with the smell of blood drove us deeper and deeper into the dark river. I became a member of the tribe, and I forgot the fields of my father.

We hunted birds with our crude weapons and battered to death stray raccoons and rabbits. Then we skinned the animals and filled the air with the smoke of roasting meat. The tribe was pleased with me and welcomed me as a hunter. They prepared for my initiation.

I, Salomon, tell you this so that you may know the meaning of life and death. How well I know it now, how clear are the events of the day I killed the giant river turtle. Since that day I have been a storyteller, forced by the order of my destiny to reveal my story. I speak to tell you how the killing became a horror.

The silence of the river was heavier than usual that day. The heat stuck to our sweating skin like a sticky syrup and the insects sucked our blood. Our half-naked bodies moved like shadows in the brush. Those ahead and behind me whispered from time to time, complaining that we were lost and suggesting that we turn back. I said nothing, it was the day of my initiation, I could not speak. There had been a fight at camp the night before and the bad feelings still lingered. But we hunted anyway, there was nothing else to do. We were compelled to hunt in the dark shadows of the river. Some days the spirit for the hunt was not good, fellow hunters quarreled over small things, and still we had to start early at daybreak to begin the long day's journey which would not bring us out until sunset.

In the branches above us the bird cries were

sharp and frightful. More than once the leader lifted his arm and the line froze, ready for action. The humid air was tense. Somewhere to my left I heard the river murmur as it swept south, and for the first time the dissatisfaction which had been building within me surfaced. I cursed the oppressive darkness and wished I was free of it. I thought of my father walking in the sunlight of his green fields and I wished I was with him. But it was not so; I owed the tribe my allegiance. I would kill the first animal we encountered.

We moved farther than usual into unknown territory, hacking away at the thick underbrush; behind me I heard murmurs of dissension. Some wanted to turn back, others wanted to rest on the warm sandbars of the river, still others wanted to finish the argument which had started the night before. My father had given me an amulet to wear and he had instructed me on the hunt, and this made the leader jealous. Some argued that I could wear the amulet, while others said no. In the end the jealous leader tore it from my neck and said that I would have to face my initiation alone.

I was thinking about how poorly prepared I was and how my father had tried to help, when the leader raised his arm and sounded the alarm. A friend behind me whispered that if we were in luck there would be a deer drinking at the river. No one had ever killed a deer in the memory of our tribe. We held our breath and waited, then the leader motioned and I moved forward to see. There in the middle of the narrow path lay the biggest tortoise any of us had ever seen. It was a huge monster which had crawled out of the dark river to lay its eggs in the warm sand. I felt a

shiver, and when I breathed, the taste of copper
drained in my mouth and settled in my queasy
stomach.

The giant turtle lifted its huge head and
looked at us with dull, glintless eyes. The tribe
drew back. Only I remained facing the monster
from the water. Its slimy head dripped with
bright green algae. It hissed a warning. It had
come out of the water to lay its eggs, now it had
to return to the river. Wet, leathery eggs fresh
from the laying clung to its webbed feet, and as it
moved forward it crushed them into the sand. Its
gray shell was dry, dulled by the sun, encrusted
with dead parasites and green growth; it needed
the water.

"Kill it!" the leader cried, and at the same
time the hunting horn sounded its too-rou which
echoed down the valley. Its call was so sad and
mournful I can hear it today as I tell my story ....
Listen, Tortuga, it is now I know that at that time
I could have forsaken my initiation and de-
nounced the darkness and insanity that urged us
to the never-ending hunt. I had not listened to
my father's words. The time was not right.

"The knife," the leader called, and the knife
of the tribe was passed forward, then slipped into
my hand. The huge turtle lumbered forward. I
could not speak. In fear I raised the knife and
brought it down with all my might. Oh, I prayed
to no gods, but since then how often I have
wished that I could undo what I did. One blow se-
vered the giant turtle's head. One clean blow and
the head rolled in the sand as the reptilian body
reared back, gushing green slime. The tribe
cheered and pressed forward. They were as surprised as I was that the kill had been so swift and

clean. We had hunted smaller tortoises before and we knew that once they retreated into their shells it took hours to kill them. Then knives and spears had to be poked into the holes and the turtle had to be turned on its back so the tedious task of cutting the softer underside could begin. But now I had beheaded the giant turtle with one blow.

"There will be enough meat for the entire tribe," one of the boys cried. He speared the head and held it aloft for everyone to see. I could only look at the dead turtle that lay quivering on the sand, its death urine and green blood staining the damp earth.

"He has passed his test," the leader shouted, "he did not need the amulet of his father. We will clean the shell and it will be his shield! And he shall now be called the man who slew the turtle!"

The tribe cheered, and for a moment I bathed in my glory. The fear left me, and so did the desire to be with my father on the harsh hills where he cultivated his fields of corn. He had been wrong; I could trust the tribe and its magic. Then someone shouted and we turned to see the turtle struggling toward us. It reared up, exposing the gaping hole where the head had been, then it charged, surprisingly swift for its huge size. Even without its head it crawled toward the river. The tribe fell back in panic.

"Kill it!" the leader shouted, "Kill it before it reaches the water! If it escapes into the water it will grow two heads and return to haunt us!"

I understood what he meant. If the creature reached the safety of the water it would live again, and it would become one more of the ghosts that lurked along our never-ending path. Now there was nothing I could do but stand my ground and finish the killing. I struck at it until the knife broke on its hard shell, and still the turtle rumbled toward the water, pushing me back. Terror and fear made me fall on the sand and grab it with my bare hands. Grunting and gasping for breath I dug my bare feet into the sand. I slipped one hand into the dark, bleeding hole where the head had been and with the other I grabbed its huge feet. I struggled to turn it on its back and rob it of its strength, but I couldn't. Its dark instinct for the water and the pull of death were stronger than my fear and desperation. I grunted and cursed as its claws cut into my arms and legs. The brush shook with our violent thrashing as we rolled down the bank towards the river. Even mortally wounded it was too strong for me. At the edge of the river, it broke free from me and plunged into the water, trailing frothy blood and bile as it disappeared into the gurgling waters.

Covered with the turtle's blood, I stood numb and trembling. As I watched it disappear into the dark waters of the river, I knew I had done a wrong. Instead of conquering my fear, I had created another shadow which would return to haunt us. I turned and looked at my companions; they trembled with fright.

"You have failed us," the leader whispered. "You have angered the river gods." He raised his talisman, a stick on which hung chicken feathers, dried juniper berries and the rattler of a snake we had killed in the spring, and he waved it in front of me to ward off the curse. Then they withdrew in silence and vanished into the dark brush, leaving me alone on that stygian bank.

Oh, I wish I could tell you how lonely I felt. I

cried for the turtle to return so I could finish the kill, or return its life, but the force of my destiny was already set and that was not to be. I understand that, now. That is why I tell you my story. I left the river, free of the tribe, but unclean and smelling of death.

That night the bad dreams came, and then the paralysis ....

The wall of the bathroom stall was covered with drawings of naked men and women. Old Placido, the janitor, worked hard to keep the walls clean, but the minute he finished scrubbing off the drawings in one stall others appeared next door. The drawings were crude, hastily done outlines. The ninth graders drew them because they knew everything. But after today, Pico assured us, we would all know, and we would be real men.

THE
APPLE
ORCHARD

It was the last week of school and we were restless. Pico and Chueco ditched every chance they got, and when they came to school it was only to bother the girls and upset the teachers, otherwise they played hookey in Duran's apple orchard, the large orchard which lay between the school and our small neighborhood. They smoked cigarettes and looked at *Playboy* magazines which they stole from their older brothers.

I stayed with them once, but my father found out about it and was very angry. "It costs money to send you to school," he said. "So go! Go and learn to get ahead in this world! Don't play hookey with those tontos, they will never amount to anything."

I dragged myself to school which, in spite of the warm spring weather, had one consolation: Miss Brighton. She was the young substitute teacher who had come to replace Mr. Portales after his nervous breakdown. She was my teacher for first period English and last period study hall. The day she arrived I helped her move her supplies and books, so we became friends. I think I fell in love with her, I looked forward to her class, and I was sad when she told me she would be with us only until the end of school. She had a regular job in Santa Fe for the following year. For a few weeks my fascination with Miss Brighton grew and I was happy. During study hall I would pretend to read, but most often I would sit and stare over my book at her. When she happened to glance up she would smile at me, and sometimes she came to my desk and asked me what I was reading. She loaned me a few books, and after I read them I told her what I had found in them. Her lips curled in a smile which almost laughed and her bright eyes shone with light. I began to memorize her features, and at night I began to dream of her.

On the last day of school Pico and Chueco came up with their crazy idea. It didn't interest me at first, but actually I was also filled with curiosity. Reluctantly, I gave in.

"It's the only way to become a man," Pico said, as if he really knew what he was talking about.

"Yeah," Chueco agreed, "we've seen it in pictures, but you gotta see the real thing to know what it's like."

"Okay, okay," I said finally, "I'll do it."

That night I stole into my parents' bedroom. I had never done that before. Their bedroom was a place where they would go for privacy, and I was never to interrupt them there. My father had only told me that once. We were washing his car when unexpectedly he turned to me and said, "When your mother and me are in the bedroom you should never disturb us, understand?" I nodded. I knew that part of their life was shut off to me, and it was to remain a mystery.

Now I felt like a thief as I stood in the dark and saw their dark forms on the bed. My father's arm rested over my mother's hip. I heard his low, peaceful snore and I was relieved that he was asleep. I hurried to her bureau and opened her vanity case. The small mirror we needed for our purpose lay among the bottles of perfume and nail polish. My hands trembled when I found it. I slipped it into my pocket and left the room quickly.

"Did you get it?" Pico asked the next morning.

We met in the apple orchard where we always met on the way to school. The flowering trees buzzed with honey bees which swarmed over the thick clusters of white petals. The fragrance reminded me of my mother's vanity case, and for a moment I wondered if I should surrender the mirror to Pico. I had never stolen anything from her before. But it was too late to back out. I took the mirror from my pocket and held it out. For a moment it reflected the light which filtered through the canopy of apple blossoms, then Pico howled and we ran to school.

We decided to steal the glue from Miss Brighton's room. "She likes you," Pico said. "You keep her busy, I'll steal the glue." So we pushed our way past the mob which filled the hallway and slipped into her room.

"Isador," she smiled when she saw me at the door, "what are you doing at school so early?" She looked at Pico and Chueco and a slight frown crossed her face.

"I came for the book," I reminded her. She was dressed in a bright spring yellow, and the light which shone through the windows glistened on her dress and her soft hair.

"Of course ... I have it ready ...." I walked with

her to the desk and she handed me the book. I glanced at the title, *"The Arabian Nights."* I shivered because out of the corner of my eye I saw Pico grab a bottle of glue and stick it under his shirt.

"Thank you," I mumbled.

We turned and raced to the bathroom. A couple of eighth graders stood by the windows, looking out and smoking cigarettes. They usually paid little attention to us seventh graders so we slipped unnoticed into one of the stalls. Pico closed the door. Even in the early morning the stall was already warm and the odor bad.

"Okay, break the mirror," Pico whispered.

"Seven years' bad luck," Chueco reminded me.

"Don't pay attention to him, break it!" Pico commanded.

I took the mirror from my pocket, recalled for a moment the warm, sweet fragrance which filled my parents' bedroom, the aroma of the vanity case, the sweet scent of the orchard, like Miss Brighton's cologne, and then I looked at Pico and Chueco's sweating faces and smelled the bad odor of the crowded stall. My hands broke out in a sweat.

"Break it!" Pico said sharply.

I looked at the mirror, briefly I saw my face in it, saw my eyes which I knew would give everything away if we were caught, and I thought of the disgrace I would bring my father if he knew what I was about to do.

I can't, I said, but there was no sound, there was only the rancid odor which rose from the toilet stool. All of our eyes were glued to the mirror as I opened my hand and let it fall. It fell slowly, as if in slow motion, reflecting us, changing our sense of time, which had moved so fast that morning, into a time which moved so slowly I thought the mirror would never hit the floor and break. But it did. The sound exploded, the mirror broke and splintered, and each piece seemed to bounce up to reflect our dark, sweating faces.

"Shhhhhhhhh," Pico whispered, finger to lips.

We held our breath and waited. Nobody moved outside the stall. No one had heard the breaking of the mirror which for me had been like the sound of thunder.

Then Pico reached down to pick up three well-shaped pieces, about the size of silver dollars. "Just right!" he grinned, and handed each of us a piece. He put his right foot on the toilet seat, opened the bottle of glue and smeared the white, sticky glue on the tip of his shoe. He placed the piece of mirror on the glue, looked down and saw his sharp, weasel face reflected in it and smiled. "Fits just right!"

We followed suit, first Chueco, then me.

"This is going to be fun!" Chueco giggled.

"Hot bloomers! Hot bloomers!" Pico slapped my back.

"Now what?"

"Wait for it to dry ...."

We stood with our feet on the toilet seat, pant legs up, waiting for the glue to dry.

"Whose panties are you going to see first?" Chueco asked Pico.

"Concha Panocha's" Pico leered, "she's got the biggest boobs!"

"If they have big boobs does that mean they have it big downstairs?" Chueco asked.

"Damn right!"

"Zow-ee!" Chueco exclaimed and spit all over me.

"Shhhh!" Pico whispered. Someone had come in. They talked while they used the urinals, then they left.

"Ninth graders," Pico said.

"Those guys know everything," Chueco added.

"Sure, but after today we'll know too," Pico grinned.

"Yeah," Chueco smiled.

I turned away to escape another shower and his bad breath. The wall of the bathroom stall was covered with drawings of naked men and women. Old Placido, the janitor, worked hard to keep the walls clean, but the minute he finished scrubbing off the drawings in one stall others appeared next door. The drawings were crude, hastily done outlines. The ninth graders drew them because they knew everything. But after today, Pico had assured us, we would all know, and we would be real men.

Last year the girls didn't seem to matter to us, we played freely with them, but the summer seemed to change everything. When we came back to school the girls had changed. They were bigger, some of them began to wear lipstick and nail polish. They carried their bodies differently, and I couldn't help but notice for the first time their small, swollen breasts. Pico explained about brassieres to me. An air of mystery began to surround the girls we had once known so well.

I began to listen closely to the stories ninth grade boys told about girls. They gathered in the bathroom to smoke before class and during lunch break, and they either talked about cars or sports or girls. Some of them already dated girls, and a few bragged about girls they had seen naked. They always talked about the girls who were 'easy' or girls they had 'made,' and they laughed at us, chasing us away when we asked questions.

Their stories were incomplete, half whispered, and the crude drawings only aroused more curiosity. The more I thought about the change which was coming over us, the more troubled I became, and at night my sweaty dreams were filled with images of women, phantasmal creatures who danced in a mist and removed their veils as they swirled around me. But always I awoke before the last veil was removed. I knew nothing. That's why I gave in to Pico's idea. I wanted to know.

He had said that if we glued a small piece of mirror to our shoes we could push our feet between the girls' legs when they weren't watching, then we could see everything.

"And they don't wear panties in the spring," he said. "Everybody knows that. So you can see everything!"

"Eehola!" Chueco whistled.

"And sometimes there's a little cherry there ...."

"Really?" Chueco exclaimed. "Like a cherry from a cherry tree?"

"Sure," Pico said, watch for it, it's good luck." He reached down and tested the mirror on his shoe. "Hey, it's dry! Let's go!"

We piled out of the dirty stall and followed Pico towards the water fountain at the end of the hall. That's where the girls usually gathered because it was outside their bathroom.

"Watch me," he said daringly, then he worked his way carefully behind Concha Panocha who stood talking to her friends. She wore a very loose skirt, perfect for Pico's plan. She was a big girl, and she wasn't very pretty, but Pico liked her. Now we watched as he slowly worked his foot between her feet until the mirror was in position. Then he looked down and we saw his eyes light up. He turned and looked at us with a grin. He had seen everything!

"Perfect! Perfect!" he shouted when he came back to us. "I could see everything! Panties! Nalgas! The spot!"

"Eee-heee-heeee," Chueco laughed. "Now it's my turn!"

They ran off to try Concha again, and I followed them. I felt the blood pounding in my head and a strange excitement ran through my body. If Pico could see everything, then I could, too! I could solve the terrible mystery which had pulled me back and forth all year long. I slipped up behind a girl, not even knowing who she was, and with my heart pounding madly I carefully pushed my foot between her feet. I worked cautiously, afraid to get caught, afraid of what I was about to see. Then I peered into the mirror, saw in a flash my guilty eyes, moved my foot to see more, but all I could see was darkness. I leaned closer to her, looked closely into the mirror, but there was nothing except the brief glimpse of her white panties and then the darkness.

I moved closer, accidentally bumped her, and she turned, looking puzzled. I said excuse me, pulled back and ran away. There was nothing to see; Pico had lied. I felt disappointed. So was Chueco when we met again at the bathroom.

"They all wear panties, you liar!" Chueco accused Pico. "I couldn't see anything. One girl caught me looking at her and she hit me with her purse," he complained. His left eye was red. "What do we do now?" Chueco asked.

"Let's forget the whole thing," I suggested. The excitement was gone, there was nothing to discover. The mystery which was changing the girls into women would remain unexplained. And not being responsible for the answer was even a relief. I reached down to pull the mirror from my foot. My leg was stiff from holding it between the girl's legs.

"No!" Pico exclaimed and grabbed my arm. "Let's try one more thing!"

"What?"

He looked at me and grinned. "Let's look at one of the teachers."

"What? You're crazy!"

"No, I'm not! The teachers are more grown up than the girls! They're really women!"

"Bah, they're old hags," Chueco frowned.

"Not Miss Brighton!" Pico smiled.

"Yeah." Chueco's eyes lit up and he wiped the white spittle that gathered at the edges of his mouth. "She reminds me of Wonder Woman!" he laughed and made a big curve with his hands.

"And she doesn't wear a bra, I know, I've seen her," Pico added.

"No," I shook my head. No, it was crazy. It would be as bad as looking at my mother. Again I reached down to tear the mirror from my shoe and again Pico stopped me.

"You can't back out now!" he hissed.

"Yeah," Chueco agreed, "we're in this together."

"If you back out now you're out of the gang," Pico warned. He held my arm tightly, hard enough for it to hurt. Chueco nodded. I looked from one to the other, and I knew they meant it. I had grown up with them, knew them even before we started school, we were a gang. Friends.

"This summer we'll be the kings of the apple orchard, and you won't be able to come in," Pico added to his threat.

"But I don't want to do it," I insisted.

"Who, then?" Chueco asked and looked at Pico. "We can't all do it, she'd know."

"So let's draw," Pico said and drew three toothpicks out of his pocket. He always carried toothpicks and usually had one hanging from his lips. "Short man does it. Fair?"

Chueco nodded. "Fair." They looked at me. I nodded. Pico broke one toothpick in half, then he put one half with two whole ones in his hand, made a fist and held it out for us to draw. I lost.

"Eho, Isador, you're lucky," Chueco said.

"I, I can't," I mumbled.

"You have to!" Pico said. "That was the deal!"

"Yeah, and we never break our deals," Chueco reminded me, "as long as we've been playing together we never broke a deal."

"If you back out now, that's the end ... no, more gang," Pico said seriously. Then he added, "Look, I'll help you. It's the last day of school, right? So there's going to be a lot of noise during last period. I'll call her to my desk and when she bends over it'll be easy! She won't know!" He slapped my back.

"Yeah, she won't know!" Chueco repeated. I finally nodded. Why argue with them, I thought, I'll just put my foot out and fake it, and later I'll make up a big story to tell them in the apple orchard. I'll tell them I saw everything. I'll say it was like the drawing in the bathroom. But it wasn't that easy. The rest of the day my thoughts crashed into each other like the goats Mr. Duran sometimes lets out in his orchard. Fake it, one side said; look and solve the mystery, the other whispered. Now's your chance!

By the time I got to last period study hall I was very nervous. I slipped into my seat across the aisle from Pico and buried my head in the book Miss Brighton had lent me. I sat with my feet drawn in beneath my desk so the mirror wouldn't show. After a while my foot grew numb in its cramped position. I flipped through the pages and tried to read, but it was no use, my thoughts were on Miss Brighton. Was she the woman who danced in my dreams? Why did I always blush when I looked in her clear, blue eyes, those eyes that even now seemed to be daring me to learn their secret.

"Ready," Pico whispered and raised his hand. I felt my throat tighten and go dry. My hands broke out in a sweat. I slipped lower into my desk, trying to hide as I heard her walk towards Pico's desk.

"I want to know this word," Pico pointed.

"Contradictory," she said, "con-tra-dic-to-ry."

"Cunt-try-dick-tory," Pico repeated.

I turned and looked at her. Beyond her, through the window, I could see the apple orchard. The buzz of the bees swarming over the blossoms filled my ears.

"It means to contradict ... like if one thing is true then the other is false," I heard her say.

I would have to confess, I thought ... forgive me, father, but I have contradicted you. I stole from my mother. I looked in the mirror and saw the secret of the woman. And why shouldn't you, something screamed in my head. You have to know! It's the only way to become a man! Look now! See! Learn everything you can!

I took a deep breath and slipped my foot from beneath my desk. I looked down, saw my eyes reflected in the small mirror. I slid it quietly between her feet. I could almost touch her skirt, smell her perfume. Behind her the light of the window and the glow from the orchard were blinding. I will pull back now, won't go all the way, I thought.

"Con-tra ...." she repeated.

"Cunt-ra ...." Pico stuttered.

Then I looked, saw in a flash her long, tanned legs, leaned to get a better image, saw the white frill, then nothing. Nothing. The swirl of darkness and the secret. The mystery remained hidden in darkness.

I gasped as she turned. She saw me pull my leg back, caught my eyes before I could bury myself in the book again, and in that brief instant I knew she had seen me. A frown crossed her face. She started to say something, then she stood very straight.

"Get your books ready, the bell's about to ring," was all she said. Then she walked quickly to her desk and sat down.

"Did you see?" Pico whispered. I said nothing, but stared at a page of the book which was a blur. The last few minutes of the class passed very slowly. I thought I could even hear the clock ticking.

Then seconds before the bell rang I heard her say, "Isador, I want you to stay after school."

My heart sank. She knew my crime. I felt sick in the pit of my stomach. I cursed Pico and

Chueco for talking me into the awful thing. Better to have let everything remain as it was. Let them keep their secret, whatever it was, it wasn't worth the love I knew would end between me and Miss Brighton. She would tell my parents, everyone would know. I wished that I could reach down and rip the cursed mirror from my shoe, undo everything and set it right again.

But I couldn't. The bell rang. The room was quickly emptied. I remained sitting at my desk. Long after the noise had cleared in the school ground she called me to her desk. I got up slowly, my legs weak and trembling, and I went to her. The room felt very big and empty, bigger than I could ever remember it. And it was very quiet.

She stood and came around her desk. Then she reached down, grabbed the small mirror on my shoe and jerked it. It splintered when she pulled and cut her thumb, but she didn't cry out, she was trembling with anger. She let the pieces drop on the floor; I saw the blood as it smeared her skirt and formed red balls on the tip of her thumb.

"Why did you do it?" she asked. Her voice was angry. "I know that Pico and Chueco would do things like that, but not you, Isador, not you!"

I shook my head. "I wanted to know," I heard myself say, "I wanted to know ...."

"To know what?" she asked.

"About women ...."

"But what's there to know? You saw the film the coach showed you ... and later we talked in class when the nurse came. She showed you the diagrams, pictures!"

I could only shake my head. "It's not the same. I wanted to know how women are ... why different? How?"

She stopped trembling. Her breathing became regular. She took my chin in her hand and made me look at her. Her eyes were clear, not angry, and the frown had left her face. I felt her blood wet my chin.

"There's stories ... and drawings, everywhere ... and at night I dream, but I still don't know, I don't know anything." I cried.

She looked at me while my frustrations came pouring out, then she drew me close and put her arms around me and smoothed my hair. "I understand," she said, "I understand...but you don't need to hide and see through the mirror. That makes it dirty. There's no secret to hide...nothing to hide...."

She held me tight, I could feel her heart pounding, and I heard her sigh, as if she too was troubled by the same questions which hounded me. Then she let me go and went to the windows where she pulled shut all of the venetian blinds. Except for a ray of light streaming through the top, the room grew dark. She went to the door and locked it, turned and looked at me, smiled with a look I had never seen before, then she walked gracefully to the small elevated platform in the back of the room.

She stood in the center and very slowly and carefully she unbuttoned her blouse. She let it drop to her feet, then she undid her bra and let it fall. I held my breath and felt my heart pounding wildly. Never had I seen such beauty as I saw then in the pale light which bathed her naked shoulders and her small breasts. She unfastened her skirt and let it drop, then she lowered her panties and stepped out of them. When she was completely naked, she called me.

"Come and see what a woman is like," she smiled.

I walked very slowly to the platform. My legs trembled, and I heard a buzzing sound, the kind bees make when they are swarming around the new blossoms of the apple trees. I stood looking at her for a long time, and she stood very still, like a statue. Then I began to walk around the platform, still looking at her, noting every feature and every curve of her long, firm legs, her flat stomach with its dot of a navel, the small round behind that curved down between her legs, then rose along her spine to her hair which fell over her shoulders. I walked around and began to feel a swirling, pleasant sensation, as if I was getting drunk. I continued to hear the humming sound, perhaps she was singing, or it was the sound of the bees in the orchard, I didn't know. She was smiling, a distant, pleasant smile.

The glowing light of the afternoon slipped through the top of the blinds and rested on her hair. It was the color of honey, spun so fine I wanted to reach out and touch it, but I was content to look at her beauty. Once I had gone hunting with my uncles and I had seen a golden aspen forest which had entranced me, but even that was not as beautiful as this. Not even the summer nights, when I slept outside and watched the swirl of the Milky Way in the dark sky, could compare with the soft curves of her body. Not even the brilliant sunsets of the summer, when the light seemed painted on the glowing clouds could be as full of wonder as the light which fell on her naked body. I looked until I thought I had memorized every curve, every nook and every shadow of her body. I breathed in deep, to inhale her aroma, then when I could no longer stand the beauty of the mystery unraveling itself before my eyes, I turned and ran.

I ran out the door into the bright setting sun, a cry of joy exploding from my lips. I ran as hard as I could, and I felt I was turning and leaping in the air like one of the goats in the apple orchard.

"Now I know!" I shouted to myself. "Now I know the secret and I'll keep it forever!"

I ran through the orchard, laughing with joy. All around me the bright white blossoms of the trees shimmered in the spring light. I heard music in the radiance which exploded around me; I felt I was dreaming.

I ran around the trees and then stopped to caress them, the smooth trunks and branches reminding me of her body. Each curve developed a slope and shadow of its own, each twist was rich with the secret we now shared. The flowers smelled like her hair and reminded me of her smile. Gasping for breath and still trembling with excitement, I fell exhausted on the ground.

It's a dream, I thought, and I'll soon wake up. No, it had happened! For a few brief moments I had shared the secret of her body, her mystery. But even now, as I tried to remember how she looked, her image was fading like a dream fades. I sat up straight, looked towards the school, and tried to picture the room and the light which had fallen on her bare shoulders, but the image was fuzzy. Her smile, her golden hair and the soft curves of her body were already fading into the sunset light, dissolving into the graceful curves of the trees. The image of her body, which just a short time ago had been so vivid, was working itself into the apple orchard, becoming the shape of trunks and branches ... and her sweet fragrance blended into the damp earth-smell of the orchard with its nettles and wild alfalfa.

For a moment I tried to keep her image from fading away. Then I realized that she would fade and grow softer in my memory, and that was the real beauty! That's why she told me to look! It was like the mystery of the apple orchard, changing before my eyes even as the sun set. All the curves and shadows, and the sounds and smells were changing form! In a few days the flowers would wilt and drop, then I would have to wait until next spring to see them again, but the memory would linger, parts of it would keep turning in my mind ... then next spring I would come back to the apple orchard to see the blossoms again. I would always keep coming back, to rediscover, to feel the smoothness of flesh and bark, to smell hair and flower, to linger as I bathed in beauty. The mystery would always be there, and I would be exploring its form forever.

"Places! Places!" Miss Violet shouted. "Joseph?" she called and I stepped forward. "Mary? Who is Mary?"

"Horse!" Red answered.

"No! No! No!" Horse cried. We chased him down on the stage and knocked over a lot of props, but we finally got the beautiful robe on him.

"Horse is a virgin!" Bones called.

"Aghhhh! ¡Cabrón!" Horse started up the rope but we pulled him down.

"Horse! Horse!" Miss Violet tried to subdue him, "it's only for a little while. And no one will know. Here." She put a heavy veil on his head and tied it around his face so that it covered all except his eyes.

"Nagggghhhhh........!" Horse screamed. It was awful to hear him cry, like he was in pain.

THE CHRISTMAS PLAY

It was the day before Christmas vacation and the schoolhouse was quiet, like a tomb frozen by winter. The buses didn't come in because of the blizzard, and even most of the town kids stayed home. But Horse and Bones and the rest of the gang from Los Jaros were there. They were the dumbest kids in school, but they never missed a single day. Hell could freeze over but they would still come marching across the tracks, wrestling, kicking at each other, stomping into the classrooms where they fidgeted nervously all day and made things miserable for their teachers.

"Where are the girls?" Bones sniffed the wind wildly and plunked into a frozen desk.

"They didn't come," I answered.

"Why?"

"¡Chingada!"

"What about the play?"

"I don't know," I said and pointed to the hall where Miss Violet conferred with the other

85

teachers who had come to school. They all wore their sweaters and shivered. Downstairs the furnace groaned and made the steam radiators ping, but it was still cold.

"No play. Shit!" Abel groaned.

Miss Violet came in. "What did you say, Abel?"

"No play. Shucks."

"We can still have a play." Miss Violet sat down and we gathered around her. "If the boys play the parts ...."

We all looked at each other. The girls had set up all the stuff in the auditorium; and they had, with Miss Violet's help, composed the story about the Three Wise Men. Originally we just stood around and acted like shepherds, but now we would have to do everything because the girls stayed home.

"Yeahhhhhh!" Horse breathed on Miss Violet.

"The other teachers don't have much to do, with so many kids absent," she turned away from the inquisitive Horse, "and they would like to come to our play ...."

"Aghhhh, nooooo," Bones growled.

"We have to read all the parts," Lloyd said. He was carefully picking at his nose.

"We could practice all morning," Miss Violet said. She looked at me.

"I think it's a great idea," Red nodded his head vigorously. He always tried to help the teacher.

"¡A la veca!"

"What does that mean?" Miss Violet asked.

"It means okay!"

So the rest of the morning we sat around reading the parts for the play. It was hard be-

cause the kids from Los Jaros couldn't read. After
lunch we went to the auditorium for one quick
practice before the other teachers came in with
their classes. Being on stage scared us and some
of the boys began to back down. Bones climbed
up a stage rope and perched on a beam near the
ceiling. He refused to come down and be in the
play.

"Boooooooooo-enz!" Miss Violet called. "Come
down!"

Bones snapped down at her like a cornered
dog. "The play is for sissies!" he shouted.

Horse threw a chunk of two-by-four at him
and almost clobbered him. The board fell and hit
the Kid and knocked him out cold. It was funny
because although he turned white and was out, his
legs kept going, like he was racing someone
across the bridge. Miss Violet worked frantically
to revive him. She was very worried.

"Here." Red had gone for water which he
splashed on the Kid's face. The Kid groaned and
opened his eyes.

"¡Cabrón Caballo!" he cursed.

The rest of us were either putting on the silly
robes and towels to make us look like shepherds,
or wandering around the stage. Someone tipped
the Christ Child over and it lost its head.

"There ain't no such thing as virgin birth,"
Florence said, looking down at the decapitated
doll. He looked like a madman, with his long legs
sticking out beneath the short robe and his head
wound in a turban.

"You're all a bunch of sissies!" Bones shouted
from above. Horse aimed the two-by-four again
but Miss Violet stopped him in time.

"Go put the head on the doll," she said.

"I gotta go to the bathroom," Abel said. He held the front of his pants.

Miss Violet nodded her head slowly, closed her eyes and said, "No."

"You could be sued for not letting him go," Lloyd said in his girlish voice. He was chewing a Tootsie Roll. Chocolate dripped down the sides of his mouth and made him look evil.

"I could be tried for murder!" Miss Violet reached for Lloyd, but he ducked and disappeared behind one of the cardboard cows by the manger.

"Come on you guys, let's cooperate!" Red shouted. He had been busy trying to get everyone to stand in their places. We had decided to make everyone stand in one place during the play. It would be easier that way. Only the kings would step forth to the manger and offer their gifts.

"Places! Places!" Miss Violet shouted. "Joseph?" she called and I stepped forward. "Mary?" Who is Mary?"

"Horse!" Red answered.

"No! No! No!" Horse cried. We chased him down on the stage and knocked over a lot of props, but we finally got the beautiful robe on him.

"Horse is a virgin!" Bones called.

"Aghhhhh! ¡Cabrón!" Horse started up the rope but we pulled him down.

"Horse! Horse!" Miss Violet tried to subdue him, "It's only for a little while. And no one will know. Here." She put a heavy veil on his head and tied it around his face so that it covered all except his eyes.

"Naggggh!" Horse screamed. It was awful to hear him cry, like he was in pain.

"I'll give you an A," Miss Violet said in exasperation. That made Horse think. He had never gotten an A in anything in his life.

"An A," he muttered, his large horse jaws working as he weighed the disgrace of his role for the grade. "Okay," he said finally, "Okay. But remember, you said an A."

"I'll be your witness," Lloyd said from behind the cow.

"Horse is a virgin!" Bones sang, and Horse quit the job and we had to persuade him all over again.

"Bones is just jealous," Red convinced him.

"Come down!" Miss Violet yelled at Bones.

"Gimme an A," Bones growled.

"All right," she agreed.

He thought awhile, then yelled, "No, gimme two A's!"

"Go to ...." She stopped herself and said, "Stay up there. But if you fall and break your neck it's not my fault!"

"You could be sued by his family for saying that," Lloyd said. He wiped his mouth and the chocolate spread all over his face.

"I got to pee ...." Abel groaned.

"Horse, kneel here." Horse was to kneel by the manger and I stood at his side, with one hand on his shoulder. When I put my arm around his shoulder, Horse's lips sputtered and I thought he would bolt. His big horse-eyes looked up at me nervously. One of the cardboard donkeys kept tipping over and hitting Horse; this only served to make him more nervous. Some of the kids were stationed behind the cardboard animals to keep them up, and they giggled and kept looking around the edges at each other. They started a spit-wad game and that made Miss Violet angry.

"Please behave!" she shouted, "pleeeeeeee-z!" The Vitamin Kid had recovered and was running around the stage. She collared him and made him stand in one spot. "Kings here," she said. I guess someone had put the robe on the Kid when he was knocked out, because otherwise no one could have held him long enough to slip the robe on.

"Does everybody have copies of the play?" Red shouted. "If you have to look at the lines, keep the script hidden so the audience doesn't see ...."

"I can seeeeeee ...." It was Bones. He leaned to look down at Florence's copy of the play and almost fell off the rafter. We all gasped, but he recovered. Then he bragged," Tarzuuuuuuun, king of the jungle!" And he started calling elephants like Tarzan does in the movie, "Aghhh-uhhhh-uhhhh-uhhhhhhhhh ...."

"¡Cabrón!"

"¡Chingada!"

Everyone was laughing.

"Bones," Miss Violet pleaded. I thought she was going to cry. "Please come down."

"I ain't no sissy!" he snarled.

"You know, I'm going to have to report you to the principal ...."

Bones laughed. He had been spanked so many times by the principal that it didn't mean anything anymore. They had become almost like friends, or like enemies who respected each other. Now when Bones was sent in for misbehaving he said the principal just made him sit. Then, Bones said, the principal very slowly lit a cigarette and smoked it, blowing rings of smoke in Bones' face all the while. Bones liked it. I guess they both got a satisfaction out of it. When the cigarette was gone and its light crushed in the ashtray, Bones was excused. Then Bones went back to the

room and told the teacher he had really gotten it
this time and he promised to be a good boy and
not break any rules. But five minutes later he
broke a rule, and of course he couldn't help it because they said his brother who worked at the
meat market had brought Bones up on raw meat.

"I ain't got page five," Abel cried. His face was
red and he looked sick.

"You don't need page five, your lines are on
page two," Red told him. He was very good about
helping Miss Violet; I only wished I could help
more. But the kids wouldn't listen to me because
I wasn't big like Red, and besides there I was
stuck with my arm around Horse.

"Florence by the light ...." Tall, angelic Florence moved under the light bulb that was the star
of the east. When the rest of the lights were
turned off the light bulb behind Florence would be
the only light. "Watch your head ...."

"Everybody ready?" The three wise men were
ready. Samuel, Florence, and the Kid. Horse and
I were ready. The fellows holding up the cardboard animals were ready, and Red was ready.

"Here they come," Miss Violet whispered. She
stepped into the wings.

I glanced up and saw the screaming horde of
first graders rushing down the aisle to sit in the
front rows. The fourth and fifth graders sat behind them. Their teachers looked at the stage,
shook their heads and left, closing the doors behind them. The audience was all ours.

"I got to pee," Abel whispered.

"Shhhhhh," Miss Violet coaxed, "everybody
quiet." She hit the light switch and the auditorium darkened. Only the star of the east shone on
the stage. Miss Violet whispered for Red to be-

gin. He stepped to the center of the stage and
began his narration.

The First Christmas!" he announced loudly.
He was a good reader.

"Hey, it's Red!" someone in the audience
shouted, and everybody giggled. I'm sure Red
blushed, but he went on; he wasn't ashamed of
stuff like that.

"I got to ...." Abel moaned.

Lloyd began to unwrap another Tootsie Roll
and the cow he was holding teetered. "The cow's
moving," someone in the first row whispered.
Horse glanced nervously behind me. I was afraid
he would run. He was trembling

" ... And they were led by the star of the east
...." and here Red pointed to the light bulb. The
kids went wild with laughter. " ... So they jour-
neyed that cold night until they came to the town
of Bethlehem ...."

"Abel peed!" Bones called from above. We
turned and saw the light of the east reflecting off
a golden pool at Abel's feet. Abel looked relieved.

"¡A la veca!"

"¡Puto!"

"How nasty," Lloyd scoffed. He turned and
spit a mouthful of chewed-up Tootsie Roll. It landed on Maxie who was holding up a cardboard donkey behind us.

Maxie got up, cleaning himself. The donkey
toppled over. "¡Jodido!" he cursed Lloyd and
shoved him. Lloyd fell over his cow.

"You could be sued for that," he threatened
from the floor.

"Boys! Boys!" Miss Violet called excitedly from
the dark.

I felt Horse's head tossing at the excitement. I

clamped my arms down to hold him, and he bit my hand.

"¡Ay!"

" ... And there in a manger, they found the babe ...." Red turned and nodded for me to speak.

"I am Joseph!" I said as loud as I could, trying to ignore the sting of the horse bite, "and this is the baby's mother ...."

"Damn you!" Horse cursed when I said that. He jumped up and let me have a hard fist in the face.

"It's Horse!" the audience squealed. He had dropped the veil, and he stood there trembling, like a trapped animal.

"Horse the virgin!" Bones called.

"Boys, Bowoooo-oizz!" Miss Violet pleaded.

" .... Andthethreekingsbroughtgiftstothe-Christchild .... " Red was reading very fast to try to get through the play, because everything was really falling apart on the stage.

The audience wasn't helping either, because they kept shouting, "Is that you, Horse?" or "Is that you, Tony?"

The Kid stepped up with the first gift. "I bring, I bring ...." He looked at his script but he couldn't read.

"Incense," I whispered.

"¿Qué?"

"Incense," I repeated. Miss Violet had rear-ranged Horse's robe and pushed him back to kneel by me. My eyes were watering from his blow.

"In-sense," the Kid said and he threw the crayon box we were using for incense right into the manger and busted the doll's head again. The round head just rolled out into the center of the stage where Red stood and he looked down at it with a puzzled expression on his face.

Then the Kid stepped back and slipped on Abel's pee. He tried to get up and run, but that only made it worse. He kept slipping and getting up, and slipping and getting up, and all the while the audience had gone wild with laughter and hysteria.

" ...Andthesecondwisemanbroughtmyrrh!" Red shouted above the din.

"Meerrr, merrrrda, mierda!" Bones cried like a monkey.

"I bring myra," Samuel said.

"Myra!" someone in the audience shouted, and all the fifth graders turned to look at a girl named Myra. All the boys said she sat on her wall at home after school and showed her panties to those who wanted to see.

"Hey, Horse!"

"¡Chingada!" the Horse said, working his teeth nervously. He stood up and I pushed and he knelt again.

The Kid was holding on to Abel, trying to regain his footing, and Abel just stood very straight and said, "I had to."

"And the third wise man brought gold!" Red shouted triumphantly. We were nearing the end.

Florence stepped forward, bowed low and handed an empty cigar box to Horse. "For the virgin," he grinned.

"¡Cabrón!" The Horse jumped up and shoved Florence across the stage, and at the same time a blood-curdling scream filled the air and Bones came sailing through the air and landed on Horse.

Florence must have hit the light bulb as he went back because there was a pop and darkness as the light of the east went out.

" ... **And that's how it was on the first Christmas!**" I heard brave Red call out above the confusion and free-for-all on stage and the howling of the audience. The bell rang and everybody ran out shouting, "Merry Christmas!" "Merry Christmas!" "¡Chingada!"

In a very few moments the auditorium was quiet. Only Red and I and Miss Violet remained on the stage. My ears were ringing, like when I stood under the railroad bridge while a train went by overhead. For the first time since we came in it was quiet in the auditorium. Overhead the wind continued to blow. The blizzard had not died out.

"What a play," Miss Violet laughed, "my Lord, what a play!" She sat on a crate in the middle of the jumbled mess and laughed. Then she looked up at the empty beam and called, "Bones, come down!" Her voice echoed in the lonely auditorium. Red and I stood quietly by her.

"Shall we start putting the things away?" Red finally asked. Miss Violet looked up at us and nodded with a smile. We straightened up the stage as best we could. While we worked we felt the wind of the blizzard increase, and the skylight of the auditorium grew dark with snow.

"I think that's about all we can do," Miss Violet said. "The storm seems to be getting worse ...."

We put on our jackets, closed the auditorium door and walked down the big, empty hall. The janitor must have turned off the furnace, because there was no noise.

"This place is like a tomb," Miss Violet shivered.

It was like a tomb. Without the kids the

schoolhouse was a giant, quiet tomb with the moaning wind crying around its edges. It was strange how everything had been so full of life and funny and in a way sad, and now everything was quiet. Our footsteps echoed in the hall.

Evening came and the mourners filled the small house. Then the man who would sing the alabados arrived. His name was Lázaro, tall and gaunt like an old, giant, gnarled alamo.

Wrapped in his dusty World War I coat, he looked like an old prophet walking out of the pages of the Bible. Out of place in a world which called itself modern, he scoffed at time because his soul was timeless. He towered over the children who gathered outside the house and the power of his one good eye made them cringe and part to let him pass.

He was tattered and unshaven, prompting some to laugh at the long hair that fell like a lion's mane around his shoulders. But he had one gift. He could sing the old prayers and make God cry in Heaven.

"Oh, wash my song
into the dead man's soul,
and soak his marrow dry.
Let his eyes burst
like dying suns,
and let his blood
sweeten
my fields of corn...."

EL
VELORIO

The deep water of the canal dumped Henry in the river, and the muddy current of the river sang as it enveloped its burden. It was a high river that carried the body southward, towards the land of the sun, beyond succor, past the last blessing of las cruces, into the dissolution that lay beyond el paso de la muerte. Dams could not stop the body that rolled and turned like a golden fish returning to its home. It was not until the body found a quiet pool that wires of a jetty would reach out like death's fingers and tangle the body in their grasp. Now the cold waters rumbled with the same insanity which had once driven Henry. The sun brought out an innocent fisherman who cast his hook and snagged dead Henry's heart.

"I'm telling you, you can't open that casket!" the county coroner insisted. He shifted his cigar in his mouth and placed his hands on his hips. He stood between Rufus and the casket he had just delivered to the mortuary door. He was a big man and he knew the law which said to get rid of the remains as soon as possible. "Why, man, there's more water wrapped in that plastic bag in the casket than there is body...." He shook his head.

"My son has been returned to us for a purpose," Rufus answered calmly. "He must have a proper velorio." He looked at Montoya who stood nervously by the casket.

"I have nothing to do with this...." Montoya wrung his hands. When he heard Rufus was coming to claim the body he had called the priest. Now he turned to Father Cayo for support.

"I know how you feel," the priest said to Rufus, "but things being as they are, why don't we just say a rosary for the dearly departed and have the coroner bury him. The county has jurisdiction in these matters...."

"You will not pray at his velorio?" Rufus asked.

"Impossible!" The priest shook his head and turned away.

"Then I have no use for you," Rufus shrugged. "I will take my son home. There the living will view the dead, the rosary will be prayed, the alabados will be sung. The velorio will last all night, the body will not be left alone. Then in the morning he can be buried. It is the proper thing to do. It is all I have to give him...."

As he moved toward the casket he remembered the death of his mother. Her eyes had not closed, and in his grief his father had placed two Liberty half-dollars on her eyelids. It was the last human touch for her on earth, and he remembered. When they were ready to seal the casket, the half-dollars were removed and the eyes remained closed. His father had given him the silver coins and he had carried them ever since. Now he had to see his son's eyes, he had to be sure that death would let them close in peace. He wanted to give his son the silver pieces blessed by his mother so long ago. It would be his last remembrance.

"You cannot move this body without proper authorization!" The coroner blocked his way. In one swift movement, Rufus thrust him aside.

"I will take my son home!" Rufus' voice was stern. He nodded and Willie helped him slip the plain, welfare casket on his back. He bent like a mule and grunted, but he lifted the heavy load. He trudged away from Montoya's Mortuary bearing the crushing load to his simple home.

It was a strange procession that followed him down the winding streets of the barrio. The news of the slow cortege spread quickly and people came to their gates to see Rufus bearing his cross. Behind trudged his wife, her black shawl pulled around her head to hide her face from staring eyes. Her children followed, frightened and cringing, bewildered by the world beyond their home. Some of the old women of the barrio pulled their black shawls over their heads and left what they were doing to follow the mournful procession. One began to pray the rosary, and the refrain of Hail Marys from the chorus mixed into the dust of the street and ascended into the bright light of the afternoon.

Crispín came, and he strummed his guitar softly, a dirge for poor, dead Henry.

Rufus did not look back. He moved ahead

with a determination that would not be deterred. Once he tripped and an old man stepped forward to help him. When they had straightened the heavy casket on his back, Rufus thanked the man and continued. They understood his need to bear the weight alone. They did not speak, but their presence was a strength. When the arduous march neared the house, some of the men went ahead to set some crates on which to place the casket, then they helped Rufus lower the heavy load.

He wanted to be alone with his dead son, and so the mourners waited outside while Rufus took a crowbar and opened the coffin. The plain lid snapped open and the smell of death permeated the room. Rufus did not recognize the water-logged remains, but still a quiet sadness made him sigh. He wanted to pray, but he couldn't find the right words. Instead, he opened the plastic bag and placed two half-dollars on the sunken pits that were once Henry's eyes. Rufus smiled. His son would have two silver moons to light his way into eternity. He crossed his forehead and then sealed everything as it had been.

The women of the barrio entered and cleaned the cluttered house while Rufus and his wife sat quietly beside the coffin. They opened the windows, airing the house, and they lit a candle at the foot of the coffin. They burned incense to drive away the smell of death. One woman brought a bouquet of roses and set them on the coffin. The house was swept clean and the kitchen scrubbed so the feast of the wake could be prepared. The children of Rufus looked bewildered, but the women drew them out of their isolation and soon they too were helping.

The women worked cheerfully as they prepared food for the velorio. There should be plenty of food for the mourners who came to keep the vigil of the wake at night, so everyone helped and contributed something. The storehouse of food grew in the kitchen. Nimble fingers pressed the round tortillas that became the bread of the wake. Pots of beans were brought and their rich fragrance blended into the aroma of the roasting chile verde. The mourners brought other gifts of food. An old friend from Belén brought a goat which he butchered in the back yard, and soon there was tender carne de cabrito roasting in the oven. In Los Padillas, the blood of the lamb was saved and made into a rich blood pudding which became the gift that was offered with el pésame to Rufus and his wife. Bowls of carne adovada, skillets of red chile de ristra made by hand, and pastelitos made of dried fruit also were brought until the tables in the kitchen were heaped high with food for the mourners. Wine and whiskey were delivered so there would be plenty of drink for those who prayed and sang for Henry's place in Heaven.

Black coffee brewed on the stove. Its fragrance and the sweet scent of burning piñon wood wafted into the living room and roused Rufus from his thoughts. What the neighbors were doing for him brought tears to his eyes. He smiled and understood that tomorrow he would be Rufus again, and that the children of the barrio would taunt him as he scavenged in the alleys, and they would sing songs about his wife. Tomorrow he would withdraw once again into the shell of his solitude, and he would walk the streets of Barelas not with the weight of his son's coffin on his back, but with the burden of his loneliness. He could accept that, because what had happened to-day would make that easier to bear.

Evening came and the mourners filled the small house. Then the man who would sing the alabados arrived. His name was Lázaro, tall and gaunt like an old, giant, gnarled alamo. Wrapped in his dusty World War I coat, he looked like an old prophet walking out of the pages of the Bible. Out of place in a world which called itself mod-ern, he scoffed at time because his soul was time-less. He towered over the children who gathered outside the house and the power of his one good eye made them cringe and part to let him pass. He was tattered and unshaven, prompting some to laugh at the long hair that fell like a lion's mane around his shoulders. But he had a gift. He could sing the old prayers and make God cry in Heaven.

With his long duster-coat flowing behind him he walked quickly to the foot of the coffin and cried out, "¡Arrímense vivos y difuntos, aquí esta-mos todos juntos." His voice cracked with the es-sence of prayer and brought the mourners to their knees.

¡Oyeme Dios!" He raised his hands toward heaven and called upon the Lord to hear him. The people bowed their heads and waited for the earth to shake.

¡La voz de Dios habla por el espíritu humano, y no hay muerte en este mundo!" he cried out.

"¡Alabados sean los dulces nombres," the women responded and made the sign of the cross. None dared look up at this man who called upon the spirit of God as a companion and a friend to be with them on this night.

"Hear me, Father!" one-eyed Lázaro sang, "I have come to sing the prayers for the dead...." His voice rose sonorously in the smoke of the burning candles. "I will sit by the throne of the Lord and sing my songs for my dead brother...." He carried all of the old alabados in his heart, and he was sure that they would please the Lord. He had walked in God's path all his life, renouncing the world and its goods, and he had walked through the door of death from an old life into a new one, so he knew that God listened to him. He was a man who conversed with God, a holy man, a man who had not sinned. And when he felt God turn to listen, he threw himself on the floor and knelt before the coffin.

"Padre nuestro que 'stas en los cielos, santifi-cado sea tu nombre...." This was his prayer to the Lord, the opening lines of the drama he would re-create this night. He would sing to God and lead the chorus of women through the dark journey of the long night until they felt the presence of death and the power of God. He would drive the knowledge of death into their hearts.

"Pray for us sinners, now and at the hour of our death," the women answered the dolorous sound of Lázaro's dry voice.

He rocked on his knees and made them understand that the body itself is a coffin, and the spirit is entombed in its blood-dark flesh. He made them understand that Henry's entrapment in the dark coffin was like theirs. His dry, raspy voice in measured meter sought to draw them into the confines of the coffin so they could feel the presence of death.

Some of the men rose to stretch and go outside to urinate against the side of the house, but the women did not leave the one-eyed prophet. His deep sonorous voice took them from hymn to hymn. At times it faltered and broke the rhythm, but it never descended from the hypnotic tempo that drove them higher and higher towards a climax with death. The concentric rings of mourners became one. The flickering light of the burning candles blurred in their eyes and reminded them of the brevity of life, while the coffin made them fear eternity. The immense weight of the mystery pressed down on them, and relief was only within the meaning of the dark coffin.

The rest of the men got up and left, moving quietly into the kitchen for a cigarette and a drink, but the women remained. Children fell asleep as Lázaro reached into his vast storehouse of songs and prayers to continue the velorio, to continue the wake that became a vigil and a conversation with one's soul. Finally the sing-song of the alabados, the fatigue, the incense of the burning candles, and the essence of faith raised the mourners to a climax where all emotions became one. There was a union with the rotting flesh in the sealed casket, and the illusion of life fell away like a veil as they made the connection with death and eternity.

Suddenly the immense weight was lifted. The woman nearest the coffin cried out, "¡Dios mío! !Dios mío!" She clutched at the casket and tried to rip away the covering. Like the others, she had been driven to a vision of eternity, and she was engulfed with pity for dead Henry.

The other women reached out to help her. A flood of tears broke loose and they cried. Relief found its way into their tired bodies. They sighed and rested their souls. They comforted each other.

Lázaro rose and went to the kitchen. His legs

felt stiff, and there was an empty feeling in his stomach. God had listened, he knew, and God had heard him. The prayers of the women were sweet to God, for He had shown them the path that Henry would walk. The Lord is good, Lázaro thought. One of the men handed him a bottle and he took a drink.

"Gracias," he acknowledged. "What time is it?"

"Past twelve, compadre," the man answered. "You prayed four hours straight...."

"Now we must eat," he said before he went outside for a breath of fresh air, "then we must pray again. We must pray until the lucero of dawn appears in the sky."

They kept the vigil until the fingers of dawn reached over the Sandia Mountains and bathed the barrio with the yellow light of the new day. They alternated prayer with eating. Bottles of wine, tequila, and whiskey were emptied, and the kitchen roared and shook with laughter. Old stories were told, gossip exchanged. Lázaro's songs and prayers heightened their awareness of death, so they celebrated the brevity of life.

That was why Rufus had carried the coffin through the streets, back to his home so his son could have a proper velorio which would entitle the dead and the living to a proper burial.

"It's cold," I answer lamely and stumble across the road to Sabrina's house. It's a large house, and it's always full of relatives. Everyone who comes from the llano, that strange ocean of plain which keeps haunting me, stops to visit us. There's already a whiff on the llano that I'm a writer, so people poke around to see where they fit into my stories. Sabrina has many visitors because her family is large. And each one of them is an emaciated storyteller. Gaunt people with dark eyes set in deep sockets, they brood with their dark secrets. But they're lousy storytellers, I think, a bunch of liars.

"Don't talk nasty about people," my wife says over my shoulder.

I have to, in order to write stories, I think. Who wants to read about saints?

A
STORY

Cast of Characters as created by the writer:

The Writer...................... myself

My Wife............................ herself

Sabrina............................ Grandpa's daughter

Sabrina's Husband........ a foreigner

Federico........................... Grandpa's son

Federico's wife...............

Grandpa............................ Don Francisco Gomez

Alfredo.............................. Grandpa's nephew

Don Cosme del Rincón......My dead uncle who
                                  wants to be a
                                  character.

Others.....................................Characters on the
                                  periphery who
                                  also want to get
                                  into the story.

TIME: It is late New Year's morning.

PLACE: My writing room.

SITUATION: I am trying to cure a hangover with a dose of New Year's football games and left over stale beer that tastes like sudsy water. I belch. Dandy Don smiles at me and reminds me the eyes of Texas are upon me. I remember a hangover remedy my uncle Cosme used to concoct when he was alive.

"Poke a hole in one side of the egg, put some salt and tabasco sauce in it, and stir it with a toothpick," he says from somewhere over my shoulder.

"It's not your story, Uncle," I remind him and frown. He's been trying to get into a story since last week, when I remembered the story my father told me about my uncle Cosme's death. But my head is too full of cobwebs to remember the details.

"Who are you talking to?" my wife calls from upstairs.

"The TV," I answer.

"I can't write today," I mumble to myself as I drag into the kitchen. "I need another situation. Real characters...." I find a nice lopsided, speckled egg in the fridge, poke a hole in it, pour in salt and tabasco sauce and mix. The phone rings.

"Phone's ringing," I call to my wife, then suck at the egg. Only the hot sauce keeps me from emptying my queasy stomach.

"Damn Uncle, I don't know what's worse, the hangover or the cure...." I shudder and return to my room to sit at my typewriter. My uncle smiles. The paper stares at me.

Menudo, the Breakfast of Champions, I write, is a sure cure for a hangover.

"It's Sabrina!" my wife calls. "She wants us to come over for menudo!"

Great, I think, the situation is improving. It's just what I needed, a new situation for a story. Then I remember last night's party. Slinky Sabrina kept throwing herself all over me, swearing I was the best writer she ever knew. The situation became, uh, sticky, uncomfortable. I erase quickly with Liquid Paper Correction Fluid and I shout "No!" but it's too late.

MENUDO, THE BREAKFAST OF CHAMPIONS has already become **A Story.**

"We'll be right over, Sabrina," my wife says into the phone, "as soon as we can get ready."

"I don't want to go!" I shout. Sabrina and her husband live across the street in an old, rambling adobe house. He's a foreigner, a German, I think. He's the quiet type; he likes to pierce you with his cold analytic eyes. Sabrina grew up in my hometown, left, some say, because she got pregnant, wandered around the world and found the German. They're both okay, but what I can't stand is her family. They are the greatest liars in the world. They love to make up stories. Awful stories! I can never think when I'm around people who tell stories.

"Ready," my wife smiles.

"What happened at the party last night?"

"You should know; you were there."

Perhaps it wasn't as bad as I thought, I reassure myself. I drank one too many, I remember. We lean into the cold, January wind. It comes down like, like, a wolf on the fold....

"That's awful!" my wife says.

"It's cold," I answer lamely and stumble across the road to Sabrina's house. It's a large house, and it's always full of relatives. Everyone who comes from the llano, that strange ocean of plain which keeps haunting me, stops to visit us. There's already a whiff on the llano that I'm a writer, so people poke around to see where they fit into my stories. Sabrina has many visitors because her family is large. And each one of them is an obsessive storyteller. Gaunt people with dark eyes set in deep sockets, they brood with their dark secrets. But they're lousy storytellers, I think, a bunch of liars.

"Don't talk nasty about people," my wife says over my shoulder.

I have to in order to write stories, I think. Who wants to read about saints? I remember my uncle Cosme del Rincón. What's the story he's trying to tell me? The wind moans and swirls dust. Suddenly Sabrina's house looms before us. The curtains are pulled and eyes stare at me from the windows. I have the feeling that I shouldn't have come. Perhaps I should go back and start all over.

"No," my wife says and knocks. Sabrina opens the door. She's dressed in a dark, revealing morning gown. "I'm so glad you came!" She smiles and throws her arms around me. "Happy New Year! Happy New Year!" I glance at my wife. What a character, she's thinking.

"We're glad we came, too," my wife smiles. There's a hug for her.

"Yes, so glad...come in, come in. Everything's fine. Oh, that was a great party last night!"

"Yes, it was nice...."

"Come in...."

"Yes."

We enter and Sabrina leads us to the den. It's a dark, subterranean room. Sabrina stumbles in the dark. She's already been nipping, I think. I take off my sheepskin jacket and look around. Good place for a scene. There are shadows wandering around the dark corners of the room, lurking at the story's edge. Sabrina reaches for two and brings them into the light.

"This is my brother, Federico, and his wife...they just came in from Tucumcari last night, well you know, they were at the party!"

There are greetings and abrazos for everyone as we're introduced. I remember somewhere I wrote: ...there's something rotten in Tucumcari. I look closely at Federico, but I can't remember him from anywhere. Federico looks closely at me. Sabrina's husband serves us sherry. "Want to play a game of billiards?" he asks and stares at me.

"No, thanks." I refuse and pick a chair where I can observe all the action. A writer always sits where he can observe the action. "Want to arm wrestle?" he asks, and I refuse again. He draws back into the shadows; I know he'll keep his eyes on me, though. I look at Federico.

"Good party last night," he nods, "but I think this neighborhood is going to the dogs."

"Someone threw a rock at him last night," his wife explains.

"It's my story!" he growls at her. "I'll tell it!" He moves dramatically to the middle of the circle. Center stage. Even the shadows that circle around us turn to listen. I nod and Federico begins his story.

"I was driving home from the party last night," he begins. I don't remember him from the party.

"Alone?" I ask.

"That's what I'd like to know!" He glares at me and sips his beer. His drooping mustache glistens with droplets of beer. The dim, overhead light makes his eyes look menacing. "That rock hit my window like an explosion!" he shouts. "There was flying glass all over!"

"Did you call the police?" Sabrina asks. She sips her sherry and swings a long, sleek leg for attention. I think she wants to get into the storytelling. Her husband clears his throat and leans over to whisper in my ear, "Federico thinks his wife was out with someone last night ... he came from the party and didn't find her home."

"There were two cops just down the street!" Federico struggles to retain my interest in his story. "They were waiting for me! But I was drunk, so...."

"Was it a real rock?" I ask.

"You should know!" he answers sharply. "It was thrown so hard it shattered the entire window! There was glass all over! It could've killed me," he whispers *sotto voce*, for dramatic emphasis, but I'm not interested. It's a dull story. I know Sabrina's kin, they're all exaggerators, liars, storytellers.

"He could've been killed!" Sabrina gasps.

"He's too mean to kill," Federico's wife snickers.

"She's got a big insurance policy on him," Sabrina whispers to my wife, "he drinks a lot...."

Sabrina's husband serves more sherry. Federico stalks off for a beer. Sabrina looks at me; she wants to begin her story.

"I wrecked my car before the party," she laughs. "I was at the beauty shop, getting all dolled up for that wild party last night, when who

do you suppose called me and wanted a ride?"
Her legs swing with mean intent. She looks at
me. Don't look at me, I think.

Federico returns and fights to keep his position at the center of the stage. "I jumped out of
the truck and looked around, but it was too dark.
I couldn't see anything except the two cops down
the street, drinking coffee while innocent drunk
people are getting their windows smashed! Oh, I
got madder than hell! I'm going to go home and
get my guns and kill this sonofabeech that's
throwing rocks, I said to myself!" He looks at
me.

"He's got a lot of guns," his wife nods at me.

"I jumped out of my chair at the beauty shop
and ran to my car to pick up whoever called me!"
Sabrina says. They're both working with a mystery element which keeps us listening, but the
stories aren't very interesting. Soap opera, I
think. Who threw the rock that bopped Federico? Who called Sabrina for a ride just before the
party started? For these and more answers, tune
in tomorrow for another exciting episode in AS
THE SPIRIT MOVES US! Organ music. Fade out.

"I'm going home," I say. My wife agrees.

"Stay for menudo!" Sabrina insists. "Grandpa's
coming soon. Stay and meet him! I know he
wants to meet you. He's a great storyteller! I
swear, you won't believe a word he says!"

"Is Grandpa coming?" Federico asks. He
peers into the shadows.

Grandpa, Don Francisco Gomez, was in the
story we began at the party last night, I remember. That's where all this started.

"Yes," Grandpa speaks from the shadows, "and
I have a story to tell...."

I feel goose pimples spread along my back. "Not yet, Grandpa," I say and turn to Federico. "Did you save the rock for fingerprints?" I ask.

"Yes, I saved the rock!" Federico nods and juts his face in front of mine. "I'm not dumb!" He spews beer-breath all over me. "I saved that rock, and I'm goin' to find out who threw it, an', an' in case you don't know it," he said threateningly, "there's a dead cat on the street!" He nods for emphasis and staggers a little.

"Federico ran over a cat last week," his wife explains.

"Maybe that's why someone is throwing rocks at you!" Sabrina laughs. We all laugh.

"Yeah, dead pussy!" Federico exclaims.

"There's a lot of stories been told about dead pussy," Grandpa adds as he enters. "But jours is by far dee worse one I eber hear!" he says with his fake accent.

Grandpa is a small, wiry man. He wears boots, a leather jacket and a cowboy hat. There's a twinkle in his eyes that can suddenly turn into a threatening flash. I feel uncomfortable with him, but it's too late to do anything about it; he's pushed his way in. Alfredo, his nephew, follows him.

"Grandpa!" Sabrina jumps up to greet her father. "When did you get here? Never mind, we're glad you're here." She hugs him. "You're just in time for a drink, then we're going to eat menudo...."

I remember that it was menudo that got me into this situation. Everyone rises to greet Grandpa. Sabrina introduces me as a writer.

"Don Francisco Gomez, a sus ordenes," Grandpa says and shakes my hand. I wince under the grip of a man who has chopped a lot of wood in his time. I feel the bones in my hand cracking. Grandpa looks into my eyes; he recognizes me from somewhere.

"My writing hand...." I smile weakly and withdraw it from his grip.

"So jew are a righter, huh?" He smiles. He has yellow teeth stained from tobacco. He wears a red kerchief tied around his neck. When he greets my wife he bows low and says, "Enchanted, Miss...." He kisses her hand. A real ham, I think. But then I've met enough of Sabrina's family to know they're all like that. Now I know they got it from the old man.

"I'm glad to meet you," my wife smiles. Grandpa winks.

Federico continues with his story. He's desperate now. "I ran ober dat cat a week ago," he slurs his words. "So last night they were waiting for me, right? I killed their pussy so they wanted to get even...."

"Federico, jew neber deed know how to tell a story. Dat dead pussy story, eet stink!" Grandpa says and moves toward center stage, threatening Federico; it's obvious Grandpa came to tell a story.

It's then that I remember Federico from the party. He came late. Stayed in a corner and drank to himself. But did he come before or after the rock-throwing incident? And was he looking for me? I look at his wife. She smiles.

"Let me tell jew a real story," Grandpa smiles, a cold glint in his eyes. He looks at me for approval. He sips his bourbon.

"Grandpa, we were talking about you last night, at the party!" Sabrina exclaims. "About the time you saw Don Cosme del Rincón murdered! Don Cosme was...." She points at me but Federico interrupts.

"I know the pussy was dead. I ran over it. I whammed it myself!" he shouts. "But I don't know who that pussy belongs to. I was too drunk," he admits and looks at his wife. "Maybe I was just thinking about dead pussy ... but I could smell it." He shakes his head sadly. "But why did the rock hit my window at that exact spot? At that exact time?"

"It always happens like that," Sabrina insists. "The right situation requires the right time, that's what Grandpa always said." Grandpa nods. He's still looking at me. "Look what happened to me when I'm driving to meet my friend!" She emphasizes "my friend" and swings her legs. "I'm driving down Central, and I know it's very crowded at 5 o'clock, so I decide to take Lomas, and it's exactly at the moment that I decide to change streets that the other car hits me! Wham, just like that! Has that ever happened to you?" she asks.

"No," I answer. "So you never got to your friend, the one who called for a ride?"

"No," she pouts and downs the remainder of her sherry. I feel easier.

"So I decided to take the law into my own hands!" Federico continues. "I went home to get my guns."

"He's got a closet full of guns," his wife nods.

Sabrina whispers to my wife: Federico shot a man once. He's very jealous. He came home late from work one night and found a man leaving his house, so he shot him. Turned out to be a poor telegraph boy just delivering a telegram." She laughs. My wife looks at me as if to say be careful with these characters. I shrug.

"I know who murder' Don Cosme del Rincón,"

Grandpa nods and begins his story. "I hab dee gun dat kill heem...."

Cut the cheap theatrics, I think. Grandpa grins and drops his accent. "The first gun I ever owned was an old Smith and Wesson .38. I was just a kid, 1914, and I was herding sheep on the Rincón llano when three men who had just escaped from the Santa Fe Prison rode into our camp...."

Sabrina claps her hands. "But *he's* from that llano, from the Rincón!" She points at me. "He's a writer! He writes stories! And Don Cosme was his uncle!"

"Ah, I thought so," Grandpa nods. The twinkle in his eyes has changed to a cold, piercing stare. "I thought I recognized you," he says, "the chin, the nose."

"Jew right books, huh?" Federico asks. He has acquired Grandpa's accent; he thinks I'm interested in the accent instead of the story.

"Yes," I say and stand to leave. "But I'm tired, I think we should leave." I look at my wife. She nods agreement. It's hard to observe a potential story if the characters know the writer is present; it causes too many interferences. The characters start acting and hamming it up, looking for a part.

"You can't go until I show you the pistol," Grandpa says sternly. "Go get the pistol, Alfredo!" he orders and Alfredo disappears into the shadows. "You know, they're writing a book about me, too," he says. His eyes bore into mine. "All those years I spent working on the llano, I saw a lot, there's a lot of stories I can tell...." He turns and walks to center stage. His presence holds our attention. The room grows silent. This is the silence before the story begins, the most challenging part of the story. The silence is ominous. From it will come the words that will affect all of us. I shiver, lean forward and wait. Alfredo returns with the pistol. The small Smith and Wesson curls like a black snake into Grandpa's hand.

"Three men escaped from prison," Grandpa begins. His words hypnotize us, rivet us to our spots. I have to give Grandpa credit, when he drops the cheap theatrics he's a real story teller. There's an aura around him, as if he's infused with the spirit of the past. "One of the escaped prisoners was a Mexican nationalist, and he was shot and killed by a deputy sheriff from Pastura. That man's family later sent many sons across the border to avenge the death, and for years the llano was filled with bloodshed ... but that's another story. The other man was a dirt farmer who didn't know his way in the llano, so there's no need to speak of him. The third man...."

"The third man was the man who killed my uncle Cosme," I interrupt. I feel a cold sweat on my forehead. So this is what my uncle Cosme was trying to warn me about! That's why he keeps appearing at the edges of my story! But what were the details of that story? I ask myself. Why am I on dangerous ground with Grandpa?

"Uncle?" I say.

My uncle Cosme struggles forward. He is a terrible sight. He has been dead for half a century. He is moldy from the grave, but I can still make out the bullet hole in his forehead. He wants to speak, he wants to warn me, but there is only a dry, raspy rattle as Grandpa pushes him back into the shadows.

"It's my story," Grandpa insists, "and I haven't finished it yet." He has grown very strong. His knuckles are white around the pistol as he points it my way. He grins. "The third man was my brother," he says, "and he returned to kill your uncle who had stolen his woman. I was herding sheep for your uncle when they rode in. At first I didn't recognize my older brother. Then he shot Don Cosme del Rincón and he gave me the pistol and he told me to hide it. I've kept it ever since. I needed to keep it because after that killing a war broke out on the llano. There was no mercy when the family honor was violated. Blood called for blood...."

"So you deserve what you get," Federico nods drunkenly.

I know, I think. I had been told that story a hundred times, but I had forgotten it. I thought I had left the past behind. I thought I had left the family feuds of the llano behind me, and now they had returned to trap me, perhaps to kill me. My legs feel weak. I look at Grandpa pointing the pistol at me.

"It must have been you who called," Sabrina says, "you're the only one I could tell my story to...."

Over my shoulder I hear Sabrina's husband whisper, "You would have been better off playing cards with me, a simple game to pass the time. Now look at the situation you've gotten yourself into."

It was a situation I was looking for, I think. I needed a story, I needed to create a situation. I see the typewriter paper in front of me and secretly yearn to recreate the past. I wish I could undo what I have done. I look at Grandpa. I know I've created my own destruction. He's an old man, and he's still avenging the old feud. I can see blood in his narrow eyes.

"Grandpa, don't point the gun!" Federico's wife cries nervously.

"Don't, Grandpa!" Sabrina cries.

"No!" my wife shouts and jumps between Grandpa and me.

There is a profound silence; the cold wind whistles around the edges of the house. The shadows shrink back into the dark corners. Then Grandpa smiles. He tosses the small pistol at me and I catch it. "It's not loaded," he says, "I just wanted you to see it. It's a beauty, isn't it? And it did so much killing in its time. But that's over now...."

Yes, I nod and look at the small, black pistol nestled in my hand, that's over now. My wife slips her arm around my waist. I look at her. Her presence is reassuring. I think she's the only one who understands what I go through with my crazy characters.

"Oh, Grandpa, you're such a joker," Federico's wife smiles.

"It's not fair to use stuff like that when you tell a story," Federico says lamely.

"Okay, enough of this nonsense, enough of this story telling!" Sabrina announces. "It's time to eat menudo! That's why all of you were invited, for a good meal of spicy menudo! And I've got hot chile and beans...." She takes her husband's arm and leads us into the kitchen.

I feel my wife take my hand. "You ready to eat?" she asks.

"Yeah," I nod.

"How's the situation?" she smiles back

"I think I've got it under control," I say. I look at Grandpa. "That's a good story," I tell him.

His eyes twinkle. "There's a lot of stories that

happened on the llano," he says. "I've never told too many of them, but now one of my grand-daughters has gotten her college degree, and she wants to write down my stories. So why not?" he chuckles.

"Hey," Federico asks as we enter the kitchen, "maybe someday you'll want to write down my story, huh? I could tell you about the time we went hunting up in the Pecos...."

"I moved closer, and when I parted the bushes I saw Don Francisco. He was sitting on a rock, and he was crying. From time to time he looked at the ravine in front of him, the hole seemed to slant into the earth. .... I looked into the pozo, and you wouldn't believe what I saw."

He waited, so I asked, "What?"

"Money! Huge piles of gold and silver coins! Necklaces and bracelets and crowns of gold, all loaded with all kinds of precious stones. Jewels! Diamonds! .... More money than I have ever seen! A fortune, my friend, a fortune which is still there, just waiting for two adventurers like us to take it!"

B. TRAVEN IS ALIVE AND WELL IN CUERNAVACA

I didn't go to Mexico to find B. Traven. Why should I? I have enough to do writing my own fiction, so I go to Mexico to write, not to search out writers. B. Traven? you ask. Don't you remember *The Treasure of the Sierra Madre*? A real classic. They made a movie from the novel. I remember seeing it when I was a kid. It was set in Mexico, and it had all the elements of a real adventure story. B. Traven was an adventurous man, traveled all over the world, then disappeared into Mexico and cut himself off from society. He gave no interviews and allowed few photographs. While he lived he remained unapproachable, anonymous to his public, a writer shrouded in mystery.

He's dead now, or they say he's dead. I think he's alive and well. At any rate, he has become something of an institution in Mexico, a man honored for his work. The cantineros and taxi drivers in Mexico City know about him as well as the cantineros of Spain knew Hemingway, or they claim to. I never mention I'm a writer when I'm in a cantina, because inevitably some aficionado will ask, "Do you know the work of B. Traven?" And from some dusty niche will appear a yellowed, thumb-worn novel by Traven. Then if the cantinero knows his business, and they all do in Mexico, he is apt to say, "Did you know that B. Traven used to drink here?" If you show the slightest interest, he will follow with, "Sure, he used to sit right over here. In this corner...." And if you don't leave right then you will wind up hearing many stories about the mysterious B. Traven while buying many drinks for the local patrons.

Everybody reads his novels, on the buses, on street corners, and if you look closely you'll spot one of his titles. One turned up for me, and that's how this story started. I was sitting in the train station in Juarez, waiting for the train to Cuernavaca, which would be an exciting title for this story except that there is no train to Cuernavaca. I was drinking beer to kill time, the erotic and sensitive Mexican time which is so different from the clean-packaged, well-kept time of the Americanos. Time in Mexico is at times cruel and punishing, but it is never indifferent. It permeates everything, it changes reality. Einstein would have loved Mexico because there time and space are one. I stare more often into empty space when I'm in Mexico. The past seems to infuse the present, and in the brown, wrinkled faces of the old people one sees the presence of the past. In Mexico I like to walk the narrow streets of the cities and the smaller pueblos, wandering aimlessly, feeling the sunlight which is so distinctively Mexican, listening to the voices which call in the streets, peering into the dark eyes which are so secretive and so proud. The Mexican people guard a secret. But in the end, one is never really lost in Mexico. All streets lead to a good cantina. All good stories start in a cantina.

At the train station, after I let the kids who hustle the tourists know that I didn't want chewing gum or cigarettes, and I didn't want my shoes shined, and I didn't want a woman at the moment, I was left alone to drink my beer. Lukecold Dos Equis. I don't remember how long I had been there or how many Dos Equis I had finished when I glanced at the seat next to me and saw a book which turned out to be a B. Traven novel, old and used and obviously much read, but a novel nevertheless. What's so strange about finding a B. Traven novel in that dingy little corner of a bar in the Juarez train station? Nothing, unless you know that in Mexico one never finds anything. It is a country that doesn't waste anything, everything is recycled. Chevrolets run with patched up Ford engines and Chrysler transmissions, buses are kept together, and kept running, with baling wire and home-made parts, yesterday's Traven novel is the pulp on which tomorrow's Fuentes story will appear. Time recycles in Mexico. Time returns to the past, and the Christian finds himself dreaming of ancient Aztec rituals. He who does not believe that Quetzalcoatl will return to save Mexico has little faith.

So the novel was the first clue. Later there was Justino. "Who is Justino?" you want to know. Justino was the jardinero who cared for the garden of my friend, the friend who had invited me to stay at his home in Cuernavaca while I contin-

ued to write. The day after I arrived I was sitting
in the sun, letting the fatigue of the long journey
ooze away, thinking nothing, when Justino appeared on the scene. He had finished cleaning
the swimming pool and was taking his morning
break, so he sat in the shade of the orange tree
and introduced himself. Right away I could tell
that he would rather be a movie actor or an ad-
venturer, a real free spirit. But things didn't work
out for him. He got married, children appeared,
he took a couple of mistresses, more children appeared, so he had to work to support his family.
"A man is like a rooster," he said after we talked
awhile, "the more chickens he has the happier he
is." Then he asked me what I was going to do
about a woman while I was there, and I told him I
hadn't thought that far ahead, that I would be happy if I could just get a damned story going.

This puzzled Justino, and I think for a few
days it worried him. So on Saturday night he took
me out for a few drinks and we wound up in some
of the bordellos of Cuernavaca in the company of
some of the most beautiful women in the world.
Justino knew them all. They loved him, and he
loved them.

I learned something more of the nature of
this jardinero a few nights later when the heat
and an irritating mosquito wouldn't let me sleep. I
heard music from a radio, so I put on my pants
and walked out into the Cuernavacan night, an oppressive, warm night heavy with the sweet perfume of the dama de la noche bushes which lined
the wall of my friend's villa. From time to time I
heard a dog cry in the distance, and I remembered that in Mexico many people die of rabies.
Perhaps that is why the walls of the wealthy are

always so high and the locks always secure. Or maybe it was because of the occasional gunshots which explode in the night. The news media tells us that Mexico is the most stable country in Latin America, and with the recent oil finds the bankers and the oil men want to keep it that way. I sense, and many know, that in the dark the revolution does not sleep. It is a spirit kept at bay by the high fences and the locked gates, yet it prowls the heart of every man. "Oil will create a new revolution," Justino had told me, "but it's going to be for our people. Mexicans are tired of building gas stations for the Gringos from Gringolandia." I understood what he meant: there is much hunger in the country.

I lit a cigarette and walked toward my friend's car which was parked in the driveway near the swimming pool. I approached quietly and peered in. On the back seat with his legs propped on the front seat-back and smoking a cigar sat Justino. Two big, luscious women sat on either side of him, running their fingers through his hair and whispering in his ears. The doors were open to allow a breeze. He looked content. Sitting there he was that famous artist on his way to an afternoon reception in Mexico City, or he was a movie star on his way to the premiere of his most recent movie. Or perhaps it was Sunday and he was taking a Sunday drive in the country, towards Tepoztlan. And why shouldn't his two friends accompany him? I had to smile. Unnoticed I backed away and returned to my room. So there was quite a bit more than met the eye to this short, dark Indian from Ocosingo.

In the morning I asked my friend, "What do you know about Justino?"

"Justino? You mean Vitorino."

"Is that his real name?"

"Sometimes he calls himself Trinidad."

"Maybe his name is Justino Vitorino Trinidad," I suggested.

"I don't know and I don't care," my friend answered. "He told me he used to be a guide in the jungle. Who knows? The Mexican Indian has an incredible imagination. Really gifted people. He's a good jardinero, and that's what matters to me. It's difficult to get good jardineros, so I don't ask questions."

"Is he reliable?" I wondered aloud.

"As reliable as a ripe mango," my friend nodded.

I wondered how much he knew, so I pushed a little further. "And the radio at night?"

"Oh, that. I hope it doesn't bother you. Robberies and break-ins are increasing here in the colonia. Something we never used to have. Vitorino said that if he keeps the radio on low the sound keeps thieves away. A very good idea, don't you think?"

I nodded. A very good idea.

"And I sleep very soundly," my friend concluded, "so I never hear it."

The following night when I awakened and heard the soft sound of the music from the radio and heard the splashing of water, I had only to look from my window to see Justino and his friends in the pool, swimming nude in the moonlight. They were joking and laughing softly as they splashed each other, being quiet so as not to awaken my friend, the patrón who slept so soundly. The women were beautiful. Brown skinned and glistening with water in the moonlight they reminded me of ancient Aztec maidens, swimming around Chac, their god of rain. They teased Justino, and he smiled as he floated on a rubber mattress in the middle of the pool, smoking his cigar, happy because they were happy. When he smiled the gold fleck of a filling glinted in the moonlight.

"¡Qué cabrón!" I laughed and closed my window.

Justino said a Mexican never lies. I believed him. If a Mexican says he will meet you at a certain time and place, he means he will meet you sometime at some place. Americans who retire in Mexico often complain of maids who swear they will come to work on a designated day, then don't show up. They did not lie, they knew they couldn't be at work, but they knew to tell the señora otherwise would make her sad or displease her, so they agree on a date so everyone would remain happy. What a beautiful aspect of character. It's a real virtue which Norteamericanos interpret as a fault in their character, because we are used to asserting ourselves on time and people. We feel secure and comfortable only when everything is neatly packaged in its proper time and place. We don't like the disorder of a free-flowing life.

Some day, I thought to myself, Justino will give a grand party in the sala of his patrón's home. His three wives, or his wife and two mistresses, and his dozens of children will be there. So will the women from the bordellos. He will preside over the feast, smoke his cigars, request his favorite beer-drinking songs from the mariachis, smile, tell stories and make sure everyone has a grand time. He will be dressed in a tuxedo, borrowed from the patrón's closet, of course, and he will act gallant and show everyone that a man who has just come into sudden wealth should share it with his friends. And in the morning he will report to the patrón that something has to be done about the poor mice that are coming in out of the streets and eating everything in the house.

"I'll buy some poison," the patrón will suggest.

"No, no," Justino will shake his head, "a little music from the radio and a candle burning in the sala will do."

And he will be right.

I liked Justino. He was a rogue with class. We talked about the weather, the lateness of the rainy season, women, the role of oil in Mexican politics. Like other workers, he believed nothing was going to filter down to the campesinos. "We could all be real Mexican greasers with all that oil," he said, "but the politicians will keep it all."

"What about the United States?" I asked.

"Oh, I have traveled in the estados unidos to the north. It's a country that's going to the dogs in a worse way than Mexico. The thing I liked the most was your cornflakes."

"Cornflakes?"

"Sí. You can make really good cornflakes."

"And women?"

"Ah, you better keep your eyes open, my friend. Those gringas are going to change the world just like the Suecas changed Spain."

"For better or for worse?"

"Spain used to be a nice country," he winked.

We talked, we argued, we drifted from subject to subject. I learned from him. I had been there a week when he told me the story which eventually led me to B. Traven. One day I was sitting under the orange tree reading the B. Traven novel I had found in the Juarez train station, keeping one eye on the ripe oranges which fell from time to time, my mind wandering as it worked to focus on a story so I could begin to write. After all, that's why I had come to Cuernavaca, to get some writing done, but nothing was coming, nothing. Justino wandered by and asked what I was reading and I replied it was an adventure story, a story of a man's search for the illusive pot of gold at the end of a make-believe rainbow. He nodded, thought awhile and gazed toward Popo, Popocatepetl, the towering volcano which lay to the south, shrouded in mist, waiting for the rains as we waited for the rains, sleeping, gazing at his female counterpart, Itza, who lay sleeping and guarding the valley of Cholula, there, where over four-hundred years ago Cortés showed his wrath and executed thousands of Cholulans.

"I am going on an adventure," he finally said and paused. "I think you might like to go with me."

I said nothing, but I put my book down and listened.

"I have been thinking about it for a long time, and now is the time to go. You see, it's like this. I grew up on the hacienda of Don Francisco Jimenez, it's to the south, just a day's drive on the carretera. In my village nobody likes Don Francisco, they fear and hate him. He has killed many men and he has taken their fortunes and buried them. He is a very rich man, muy rico. Many men have tried to kill him, but Don Francisco is like the devil, he kills them first."

I listened as I always listen, because one never knows when a word or a phrase or an idea will be the seed from which a story sprouts, but at first there was nothing interesting. It sounded like the typical patrón-peón story I had heard so many times before. A man, the patrón, keeps the workers enslaved, in serfdom, and because he wields so much power soon stories are told about him and he begins to acquire super-human powers. He acquires a mystique, just like the divine right of old. The patrón wields a mean machete, like old King Arthur swung Excaliber. He chops off heads of dissenters and sits on top of the bones and skulls pyramid, the king of the mountain, the top macho.

"One day I was sent to look for lost cattle," Justino continued. "I rode back into the hills where I had never been. At the foot of a hill, near a ravine, I saw something move in the bush. I dismounted and moved forward quietly. I was afraid it might be bandidos who steal cattle, and if they saw me they would kill me. When I came near the place I heard a strange sound. Somebody was crying. My back shivered, just like a dog when he sniffs the devil at night. I thought I was going to see witches, brujas who like to go to those deserted places to dance for the devil, or La Llorona."

"La Llorona," I said aloud. My interest grew. I had been hearing Llorona stories since I was a kid, and I was always ready for one more. La Llorona was that archetypal woman of ancient legends who murdered her children, then repentant and demented she has spent the rest of eternity searching for them.

"Sí, La Llorona. You know that poor woman used to drink a lot. She played around with men, and when she had babies she got rid of them by throwing them into la barranca. One day she realized what she had done and went crazy. She started crying and pulling her hair and running up and down the sides of cliffs of the river looking for her children. It's a very sad story."

A new version, I thought, and yes, a sad story. And what of the men who made love to the woman who became La Llorona? Did they ever cry for their children? It doesn't seem fair to have only her suffer, only her crying and doing penance. Perhaps a man should run with her, and in our legends we would call him "El Mero Chingón," he who screwed up everything. Then maybe the tale of love and passion and the insanity it can bring will be complete. Yes, I think someday I will write that story.

"What did you see?" I asked Justino.

"Something worse than La Llorona," he whispered.

To the south a wind mourned and moved the clouds off Popo's crown. The bald, snow-covered mountain thrust its power into the blue Mexican sky. The light glowed like liquid gold around the god's head. Popo was a god, an ancient god. Somewhere at his feet Justino's story had taken place.

"I moved closer, and when I parted the bushes I saw Don Francisco. He was sitting on a rock, and he was crying. From time to time he looked at the ravine in front of him, the hole seemed to slant into the earth. That pozo is called el Pozo de Mendoza. I had heard stories about it before, but I had never seen it. I looked into the pozo, and you wouldn't believe what I saw."

He waited, so I asked, "What?"

"Money! Huge piles of gold and silver coins! Necklaces and bracelets and crowns of gold, all loaded with all kinds of precious stones! Jewels! Diamonds! All sparkling in the sunlight that entered the hole. More money than I have ever seen! A fortune, my friend, a fortune which is still there, just waiting for two adventurers like us to take it!"

"Us? But what about Don Francisco? It's his land, his fortune."

"Ah, " Justino smiled, "that's the strange thing about this fortune. Don Francisco can't touch it, that's why he was crying. You see, I stayed there, and I watched him closely. Every time he stood up and started to walk into the pozo the money disappeared. He stretched out his hand to grab the gold, and poof, it was gone! That's why he was crying! He murdered all those people and hid their wealth in the pozo, but now he can't touch it. He is cursed."

"El Pozo de Mendoza," I said aloud. Something began to click in my mind. I smelled a story.

"Who was Mendoza?" I asked.

"He was a very rich man. Don Francisco killed him in a quarrel they had over some cattle. But Mendoza must have put a curse on Don Francisco before he died, because now Don Francisco can't get to the money."

"So Mendoza's ghost haunts old Don Francisco."

"Many ghosts haunt him," Justino answered. "He has killed many men."

"And the fortune, the money...."

He looked at me and his eyes were dark and piercing. "It's still there. Waiting for us!"

"But it disappears as one approaches it, you said so yourself. Perhaps it's only an hallucination."

Justino shook his head. "No, it's real gold and silver, not hallucination money. It disappears for

Don Francisco because the curse is on him, but the curse is not on us." He smiled. He knew he had drawn me into his plot. "We didn't steal the money, so it won't disappear for us. And you are not connected with the place. You are innocent. I've thought very carefully about it, and now is the time to go. I can lower you into the pozo with a rope, in a few hours we can bring out the entire fortune. All we need is a car. You can borrow the patrón's car, he is your friend. But he must not know where we're going. We can be there and back in one day, one night." He nodded as if to assure me, then he turned and looked at the sky. "It will not rain today. It will not rain for a week. Now is the time to go."

He winked and returned to watering the grass and flowers of the jardín, a wild Pan among the bougainvillea and the roses, a man possessed by a dream. The gold was not for him, he told me the next day, it was for his women, he would buy them all gifts, bright dresses, and he would take them on a vacation to the United States, he would educate his children, send them to the best colleges. I listened and the germ of a story cluttered my thoughts as I sat beneath the orange tree in the mornings. I couldn't write, nothing was coming, but I knew that there were elements for a good story in Justino's tale. In dreams I saw the lonely hacienda to the south. I saw the pathetic, tormented figure of Don Francisco as he cried over the fortune he couldn't touch. I saw the ghosts of the men he had killed, the lonely women who mourned over them and cursed the evil Don Francisco. In one dream I saw a man I took to be B. Traven, a grey-haired, distinguished looking gentleman who looked at me and nodded approvingly.

"Yes, there's a story there, follow it, follow it...."

In the meantime, other small and seemingly insignificant details came my way. During a luncheon at the home of my friend, a woman I did not know leaned toward me and asked if I would like to meet the widow of B. Traven. The woman's hair was tinged orange, her complexion was ashen grey. I didn't know who she was or why she would mention B. Traven to me. How did she know Traven had come to haunt my thoughts? Was she a clue which would help unravel the mystery?

I didn't know, but I nodded. Yes, I would like to meet her. I had heard that Traven's widow, Rosa Elena, lived in Mexico City. But what would I ask her? What did I want to know? Would she know Traven's secret? Somehow he had learned that to keep his magic intact he had to keep away from the public.

Like the fortune in the pozo, the magic feel for the story might disappear if unclean hands reached for it. I turned to look at the woman, but she was gone. I wandered to the terrace to finish my beer. Justino sat beneath the orange tree. He yawned. I knew the literary talk bored him. He was eager to be on the way to el Pozo de Mendoza.

I was nervous, too, but I didn't know why. The tension for the story was there, but something was missing. Or perhaps it was just Justino's insistence that I decide whether I was going or not that drove me out of the house in the mornings. Time usually devoted to writing found me in a small cafe in the center of town. From there I could watch the shops open, watch the people cross the zócalo, the main square. I drank lots of coffee, I smoked a lot, I daydreamed, I wondered about the significance of the pozo, the fortune, Justino, the story I wanted to write and B. Traven. In one of these moods I saw a friend from whom I hadn't heard in years. Suddenly he was there, trekking across the square, dressed like an old rabbi, moss and green algae for a beard, and followed by a troop of very dignified Lacandones, Mayan Indians from Chiapas.

"Victor," I gasped, unsure if he was real or a part of the shadows which the sun created as it flooded the square with its light.

"I have no time to talk," he said as he stopped to munch on my pan dulce and sip my coffee. "I only want you to know, for purposes of your story, that I was in a Lacandonian village last month, and a Hollywood film crew descended from the sky. They came in helicopters. They set up tents near the village, and big-bosomed, bikinied actresses emerged from them, tossed themselves on the cut trees which are the atrocity of the giant American lumber companies, and they cried while the director shot his film. Then they produced a grey-haired old man from one of the tents and took shots of him posing with the Indians. Herr Traven, the director called him."

He finished my coffee, nodded to his friends and they began to walk away.

"B. Traven?" I asked.

He turned. "No, an imposter, an actor. Be careful for imposters. Remember, even Traven used many disguises, many names!"

"Then he's alive and well?" I shouted. People around me turned to stare.

"His spirit is with us," were the last words I heard as they moved across the zócalo, a strange troop of near naked Lacandon Mayans and my friend the Guatemalan Jew, returning to the rain forest, returning to the primal innocent land.

I slumped in my chair and looked at my empty cup. What did it mean? As their trees fall the Lacandones die. Betrayed as B. Traven was betrayed. Does each one of us also die as the trees fall in the dark depths of the Chiapas jungle? Far to the north, in Aztlan, it is the same where the earth is ripped open to expose and mine the yellow uranium. A few poets sing songs and stand in the way as the giant machines of the corporations rumble over the land and grind everything into dust. New holes are made in the earth, pozos full of curses, pozos with fortunes we cannot touch, should not touch. Oil, coal, uranium, from holes in the earth through which we suck the blood of the earth.

There were other incidents. A telephone call late one night, a voice with a German accent called my name, and when I answered the line went dead. A letter addressed to B. Traven came in the mail. It was dated March 26, 1969. My friend returned it to the post office. Justino grew more and more morose. He sat under the orange tree and stared into space, my friend complained about the garden drying up. Justino looked at me and scowled. He did a little work then went back to daydreaming. Without the rains the garden withered. His heart was set on the adventure which lay at el pozo.

Finally I said "Yes, dammit, why not, let's go, neither one of us is getting anything done here," and Justino, cheering like a child, ran to prepare for the trip. But when I asked my friend for the weekend loan of the car he reminded me that we were invited to a tertulia, an afternoon reception, at the home of Señora Ana R. Many writers and artists would be there. It was in my honor, so I could meet the literati of Cuernavaca. I had to tell Justino I couldn't go.

Now it was I who grew morose. The story growing within would not let me sleep. I awakened in the night and looked out the window, hoping to see Justino and women bathing in the pool, enjoying themselves. But all was quiet. No radio played. The still night was warm and heavy. From time to time gunshots sounded in the dark, dogs barked, and the presence of a Mexico which never sleeps closed in on me.

Saturday morning dawned with a strange overcast. Perhaps the rains will come, I thought. In the afternoon I reluctantly accompanied my friend to the reception. I had not seen Justino all day, but I saw him at the gate as we drove out. He looked tired, as if he, too, had not slept. He wore the white shirt and baggy pants of a campesino. His straw hat cast a shadow over his eyes. I wondered if he had decided to go to the pozo alone. He didn't speak as we drove through the gate, he only nodded. When I looked back I saw him standing by the gate, looking after the car, and I had a vague, uneasy feeling that I had lost an opportunity.

The afternoon gathering was a pleasant affair, attended by a number of affectionate artists, critics and writers who enjoyed the refreshing drinks which quenched the thirst.

But my mood drove me away from the crowd. I wandered around the terrace and found a foyer surrounded by green plants, huge fronds and ferns and flowering bougainvillea. I pushed the green aside and entered a quiet, very private alcove. The light was dim, the air was cool, a perfect place for contemplation.

At first I thought I was alone, then I saw the man sitting in one of the wicker chairs next to a small wrought iron table. He was an elderly white-haired gentleman. His face showed he had lived a full life, yet he was still very distinguished in his manner and posture. His eyes shone brightly.

"Perdón," I apologized and turned to leave. I did not want to intrude.

"No, no, please," he motioned to the empty chair, "I've been waiting for you." He spoke English with a slight German accent. Or perhaps it was Norwegian, I couldn't tell the difference. "I can't take the literary gossip. I prefer the quiet."

I nodded and sat. He smiled and I felt at ease. I took the cigar he offered and we lit up. He began to talk and I listened. He was a writer also, but I had the good manners not to ask his titles. He talked about the changing Mexico, the change the new oil would bring, the lateness of the rains and how they affected the people and the land, and he talked about how important a woman was in a writer's life. He wanted to know about me, about the Chicanos, of Aztlan, about our work. It was the workers, he said, who would change society. The artist learned from the worker. I talked, and sometime during the conversation I told him the name of the friend with whom I was staying. He laughed and wanted to know if Vitorino was still working for him.

"Do you know Justino?" I asked.

"Oh, yes, I know that old guide. I met him many years ago, when I first came to Mexico," he answered. "Justino knows the campesino very well. He and I traveled many places together, he in search of adventure, I in search of stories."

I thought the coincidence strange, so I gathered the courage and asked, "Did he ever tell you the story of the fortune at el Pozo de Mendoza?"

"Tell me?" the old man smiled. "I went there."

"With Justino?"

"Yes, I went with him. What a rogue he was in those days, but a good man. If I remember correctly I even wrote a story based on that adventure. Not a very good story. Never came to anything. But we had a grand time. People like Justino are the writer's source. We met interesting people and saw fabulous places, enough to last me a lifetime. We were supposed to be gone for one day, but we were gone nearly three years. You see, I wasn't interested in the pots of gold he kept saying were just over the next hill. I went because there was a story to write."

"Yes, that's what interested me," I agreed.

"A writer has to follow a story if it leads him to hell itself. That's our curse. Ay, and each one of us knows our own private hell."

I nodded. I felt relieved. I sat back to smoke the cigar and sip from my drink. Somewhere to the west the sun bronzed the evening sky. On a clear afternoon, Popo's crown would glow like fire.

"Yes" the old man continued, "a writer's job is to find and follow people like Justino. They're the source of life. The ones you have to keep away from are the dilettantes like the ones in there." He motioned in the general direction of the noise of the party. "I stay with people like Justino. They may be illiterate, but they understand our descent into the pozo of hell, and they understand us because they're willing to share the adventure with us. You seek fame and notoriety and you're dead as a writer."

I sat upright. I understood now what the pozo meant, why Justino had come into my life to tell me the story. It was clear. I rose quickly and shook the old man's hand. I turned and parted the palm leaves of the alcove. There, across the way, in one of the streets that led out of the maze of the town towards the south, I saw Justino. He was walking in the direction of Popo, and he was followed by women and children, a rag-tail army of adventurers, all happy, all singing. He looked up to where I stood on the terrace, and he smiled as he waved. He paused to light the stub of a cigar. The women turned, and the children turned, and all waved to me. Then they continued their walk, south, towards the foot of the volcano. They were going to the Pozo de Mendoza, to the place where the story originated.

I wanted to run after them, to join them in the glorious light which bathed the Cuernavaca valley and the majestic snow-covered head of Popo. The light was everywhere, a magnetic element which flowed from the clouds. I waved as Justino and his followers disappeared in the light. Then I turned to say something to the old man, but he was gone. I was alone in the alcove. Somewhere in the background I heard the tinkling of glasses and the laughter which came from the party, but that was not for me.

I left the terrace and crossed the lawn, found the gate and walked down the street. The sounds of Mexico filled the air. I felt light and happy. I wandered aimlessly through the curving, narrow streets, then I quickened my pace because suddenly the story was overflowing and I needed to write.   I needed to get to my quiet room and write the story about B. Traven being alive and well in Cuernavaca.

The Pyramid of the Magician was well preserved, white limestone framed against the flat expanse of jungle around him and the clear blue December sky. The colors reminded him of Monte Alban. Below him he could see the Ball Court, beyond the Temple of the Nuns. Impressive, yes, he thought, as Chichén Itzá or Monte Alban, but there is little magic left here .... Time passed as the hot sun moved overhead, and the tourists, who had come to see Uxmal, moved over the site like ants, pausing only to take pictures or to listen to the guides who had come with the buses and who led them around the site. Then, seeking shade, he moved down towards the trees near the Pyramid of the Magician. That's where he met Gonzalo.

"A'ra! A'ra!" he shouted, and people gathered around him. "Here we begin the best tour of Uxmal! Come with Gonzalo and learn all the history and ancient secrets of this glorious city of the Mayas!"

THE VILLAGE
WHICH THE GODS
PAINTED YELLOW

It is there, the natives whispered, just south
of Uxmal, the village which the gods painted yellow.

He heard the legend in the villages, in the
cantinas, in the mercados, the stories were told
wherever the Indians gathered, and the longer he
stayed in Yucatán the more often he heard of the
village. When the Indians spoke about the village,
their dark eyes lighted and they nodded in ac-
knowledgement, then, because he was a stranger
in their midst, they would avert their eyes and a
heavy silence would fall over their group.

It is only one more legend in the land of legends, he said to himself as he boarded the bus at
Mérida to go to Uxmal, and the stories are as
countless as the Mayan ruins which dot all of Gua-
temala and Yucatán. He found a seat by a window,
huddled into himself and closed his eyes. I have
grown tired of following the legends, he thought,
I have grown cynical in my quest.

Why, then, was he going to Uxmal? It was
late December, the day of the winter solstice. All
over Mexico and Central America there were a

hundred more interesting places he could be, villages where old ceremonies in honor of the dying sun would be re-enacted, clothed by the thin veneer of Christianity, to be sure, but he knew that at the core of every ceremony lay the same values and thought which were inherent in the original, pristine and ancient ceremony. That's what did not change, the purpose of the ceremony. The surfaces changed as the culture changed, but wrapped within the ritual he always sensed a moment of time so pregnant with meaning and power that he trembled as if he were a witness to an act of great mystery.

But the real revelation he sought in those moments of time, the miraculous epiphanies the natives experienced, had never come to him. He had seen many of the ceremonies, but always he had been only the observer, never had he felt a spiritual elation or revelation which the ceremony intended to induce.

As the bus chugged up the small, unimpressive hills near Uxmal he dozed in and out of sleep, and he dreamed again of the ancient ruins he had haunted in search of a clue to the mystery of time and life in the new world. His first trip had been to the desert ruins at Casas Grandes in northern Mexico; a year later he was at Teotihuacán where he scrambled up the Pyramid of the Sun just like all the other tourists who came in from Mexico City. But it was not really until he went to Tula that he first felt a little of the aura and mystery of that ancient, sacred place. Gradually he worked his way south into the land of the Maya, to Copán, Quiriguá, Palenque, Tikal, Tulum, Chichén Itzá ...and today, on the day of the solstice, Uxmal. Ooshmal, the very sound was like a dying breath. He gasped for air in the hot, stifling bus, sat up in the seat and peered out the window. The green jungle stretched as far as he could see. Soon they would arrive at Uxmal.

Uxmal of the ancient Mayas, temples of exqui-
site beauty and haunting power, built by a people
who had developed a superior astronomy and
mathematics.

The Mayans had clocked the precise move-
ments of the sun and moon and planets at a time
when Europe was just awakening from its dark
age. Here, on the peninsula of Yucatán, one of
those mysterious upsurges in the cycle of time
had suddenly and brilliantly illuminated the history of mankind, and then the Spaniard had come
and destroyed nearly everything. Now there were
only legends and whispers about that ancient civilization and its secrets.

The stela at Quiriguá computes time four hundred million years into the past, a feat modern
man could only achieve recently with computers
and atomic clocks. He thought about this as he
looked at the cultivated fields of sisal. Time was a
god to those people, no, not a god, an element of
life. They scanned the heavens at night, plotted
their lunar calendars, knew the exact moment of
the solstices and the equinoxes, computed astro-
nomical charts which finally meshed the movement of the planets and stars into the movement
of the birth and life of the universe itself, a spiritual possession which drove them to plot the exact
moment when life first throbbed on the planet
Earth. Was that what they had learned? Was that
year zero, moment zero, the first spark of life
coming into consciousness on a foreboding Earth?
If so, at that moment and in that place there lay a
power far beyond the understanding of any
man...there at that ceremony lies the power of the
gods.

"It is time for you to go to Uxmal," the bartender at the Hotel Isabela had said, he whose
face bore a faint resemblance to the Chinese visages carved into the stela of Copán. "Here you are

wasting your time." He nodded towards the European women, the pale Swedes and German women who fled their frigid winter for a week at Cancún or Cozumel. They came to Mérida as an afterthought, to tour Uxmal before returning to their own cold peninsula.

"Go, Rosario," the bartender had said. In the afternoons he went to the bar of the hotel to escape the dust and heat of the streets, to drink cold León Negra, and to watch the European women who came in from their tours, hot and lonely and ready for company. He went there because the bartender was Mayan, a young, handsome fellow who attracted the European women, and together they kept the women of the pale legs happy.

The bartender had been serious, and that had surprised Rosario. "Go to Uxmal," he said, "and when you go, look for Gonzalo. He knows more than any of the other guides. He will show you the greatness of the Maya. He is muy Maya."

His friend was right. He had been wasting his time drinking beer and playing around with women. He had felt trepidation, a reluctance, but that morning he had boarded the bus, seeking neither the village nor Gonzalo, seeking only, with what little faith he had left, what he had sought everywhere else, a clue which might reveal the source of the knowledge of the ancients. He skirted the gate as well as the tourists lined up at the refreshment stand, and climbed the rise near the Turtle House from where he had a clear view of the site. It was impressive.

The Pyramid of the Magician was well preserved, white limestone framed against the flat expanse of jungle around him and the clear blue December sky. The colors reminded him of Monte Alban. Below him he could see the Ball Court, beyond the Temple of the Nuns. Impres-

sive, yes, he thought, as Chichén Itzá or Monte Alban, but there is little magic left here. He stood
for a long time, hoping he would feel some vibration from the place, praying it would be more
than just an impressive reconstructed Mayan site,
desiring to feel the same power from the earth or
the heavens which the ancient builders felt when
they constructed the magnificent temple. Time
passed as the hot sun moved overhead, and the
tourists, who had come to see Uxmal, moved over
the site like ants, pausing only to take pictures or
to listen to the guides who had come with the
buses and who led them around the site. Then,
seeking shade, he moved down towards the trees
near the Pyramid of the Magician. That's where
he met Gonzalo.

"A'ra! A'ra!" Gonzalo shouted, and people gathered around him. "Here we begin the best tour of
Uxmal! Come with Gonzalo and learn all the history and ancient secrets of this glorious city of the
Mayas!" A few tourists clustered around the small,
impish man, a gnome with a crippled leg and a
hunched back. He was immaculately dressed in
the white pants and shirt of the peon. His white
hair floated about his dark face, his eyes were
black and piercing. The women flocked to him,
and he smiled and clicked his tongue and paid
them compliments. In another country he would
have been a Pan luring shepherd maidens into
hidden bowers, here he was a dwarf who led
them into the secret, shady spots of Uxmal.

"You, too," he said. "Come." He beckoned to
Rosario, drawing the young man forward with his
hypnotic eyes, speaking in a Mayan dialect which
Rosario understood. Rosario followed the impish
guide of Uxmal who shouted, "A'ra! A'ra! Follow
me, and I will disclose the secrets of Uxmal!"

And he was good, very good in his presenta-
tion. Standing at the foot of the Pyramid of the

Magician he enthralled the women in the group by telling the old story about the pyramid being built in one night, built by a dwarf who in ancient times was a magician who had great powers.

"But why was it built?" a big-bosomed, red-haired woman asked. Gonzalo smiled and answered, "To honor the gods. All this was built to honor the gods. And the people still say that the magician is not dead, he will come again to raise new pyramids to the gods!" The women oohed and ahhed while Gonzalo grinned and moved closer to one woman, a Swede, middle-aged, obviously traveling alone. "You see, my friend," Gonzalo whispered, "we know very little about the ancient Mayas. We can only speculate about their ways. But I am a descendant of the Mayan people, and I know in my blood the story of the old magician is true. Other anthropologists and archeologists have suggested that the ruins abound with symbols for the phallis, and some had gone as far as to say the Pyramid of the Magician is a phallic symbol. And is there not some truth in this? Don't all mythologies of mankind speak of the gods who have come down to Earth to visit woman and create a new race of man? And isn't man himself filled with a need to thrust his power beyond earth, an urge to call down the gods and do honor to them, their fathers?"

He grinned. The Swede smiled but moved away. She got the message but she's not interested, Rosario mused. Then, he, too, felt tired. Overhead the sun was a ball of fire. Our friend Gonzalo is a charlatan, he thought, and wondered if it would not have been better to stay in the cantina of the hotel until the fervor and tension of the solstice and the Christmas celebration in its wake were over and done with.

"A'ra!" Gonzalo shouted to keep the group together. "Come, I will show you more secrets.

Look here," he cried as he pointed at a half circle
keystone which locked an arch into place. "Other
guides will tell you the ancient Mayas did not
know the circle. But they did. See? There is a
keystone built in a half circle!"

"But why didn't they build the wheel?" asked a
thin American schoolteacher. She pushed up her
glasses which kept sliding down her nose.

"The circle is holy," Gonzalo intoned, "it is a
sacred symbol of the gods. The Mayas were wise
not to profane the circle by using its shape in a
common wheel!" The teacher nodded and took
notes. Others moved away to the refreshment
stand. Rosario remained unimpressed. He had
traveled too far and seen too much to be impressed. True, the old man was a dramatic, char-
ismatic person, one could not help but be spellbound by his strength and gestures and tone of
voice, but his anecdotes were trite. As Rosario
turned away he felt the old man's hand on his
arm.

"We are brothers under the sun," he whispered, then grinned and glanced at the women.
"They are poor, pale chickens coming to their
brown roosters, eh?"

"I didn't come to chase after women," Rosario
answered, somewhat contemptuously, but instantly felt ashamed. Hadn't he spent the past few
weeks doing exactly that?

"Why did you come to Uxmal?" Gonzalo asked,
his dark eyes piercing Rosario.

"I, I've been searching...." was all Rosario could
stammer in response. Gonzalos' eyes held him.

"Yes, I can see you have come to learn the
magic. Then follow me and I will reveal some secrets." He turned and called the group together
again, shouting, "A'ra! A'ra!" as he led them to the
ball court of Uxmal. Huge numbered stones and
lintels lay on the ground, ready to be lifted into

their original positions.

"Long before your baseball or your football were invented, the Mayans played a ball game in this court. The nobles came to watch, for the game was played in honor of the sun, the Lord of Light," Gonzalo said. "When the game was done those who had won were judged to be close to the gods, so they were made priests." He waited a moment, and when no one in the now-weary group asked about the losers he said, "And those who lost the game were judged not to be in close contact with the gods, so their hearts were cut out and offered as sacrifice to the Sun-god. That way they were really close to the gods, eh?" Gonzalo smiled.

The women nodded, Rosario shook his head in disappointment. He had heard many variations of the story. Gonzalo looked at him and scowled as he removed his straw hat and wiped his brow with a white kerchief. So, you're not impressed, his eyes seemed to say, then he, too, nervously replaced his hat and looked up as if to judge the place of the sun in the sky. A slight twitch showed under his left eye as he turned to the group.

"We are near the end of our tour," he said, a note of anxiety in his voice, the sharp sense of control gone. "From here you can go into the Temple of the Nuns, to see the faces of those ancient rulers who were really gods who came from...." He stopped, shook his head as if in pain. "Those rulers, who because of their dress are now called nuns...they were nobles of Uxmal...but here!" He whirled suddenly and leaped on one of the huge blocks of stone which was but one massive piece of the huge serpentine body that once had graced the lintel of the ball court.

"See here!" he cried. "I will tell you one more story, one that the other guides do not know. Only

I, Gonzalo de las Serpientes know it, and I will
tell it to you. This snake you see decorating the
lintel of the ball court. Who carved this master-
piece? And why? Is it enough to know that the
snake is the predominant symbol of Mesoameri-
ca? The snake copulates like men and women,
and the female gives birth to its young like a
woman.... It is a symbol of fertility."

His voice cracked, Rosario shook his head and
wished he had not come to Uxmal. The old man
knew nothing new.

"But I have my own theory," Gonzalo continued, "and I will share this secret with you." The
women of the group drew closer. "No one has
ever dared to say this, but I say it. The artisans of
the Mayan society were women! Yes, women
carved the figures in the Temple of the Nuns! And
the serpent of the ball court, that, too, was carved
by women! And do you want to know why they
carved so many snakes?" He grinned fiendishly,
drew closer as he whispered, "It's because the old
Mayans were insatiable lovers!" He tossed his
head back and chuckled.

The women shook their heads and moved
away, some walked the trail towards the Temple
of the Nuns, others back to the air-conditioned
bus for a break from the mounting heat of the day.
Only Rosario and the old man were left in the ball
court, and Rosario was not quite sure why he had
remained this long. Overhead the sun had started
its descent into the afternoon, a descent which
would complete the shortest day of the year, in
ancient times one of the most crucial days in the
solar calendar and in the religious life of the Maya.

"Come!" Gonzalo said suddenly, serious again.
"We are rid of the tourists. Now is time to do our
work." His eyes burned with a deep, intense power. Rosario didn't understand what he meant by
"our work," but he followed the old man as he

scrambled like a goat up the steep steps of the Pyramid of the Magician. "A'ra!" he shouted, "A'ra!" Rosario followed as if hypnotized.

There were no people at the top. Most had returned to the buses below. The tourists who came from Mérida liked to tour in the morning when it was cool, the afternoons, as every civilized person knew, were to be spent in the cool cantina or by the swimming pool.

"Look," he said, "Look around you. What do you see?" Beneath them the jungle and fields of sisal on the flat peninsula spread as far as the eye could see. Flat expanse and scorching blue sky, that was all there was.

"Look, see the roads?" Gonzalo pointed at the barely discernible straight lines which were like the spokes of a large wheel with Uxmal at the hub. Now covered by jungle and leveled by fields they were barely visible, straight lines which showed only because at one time they had been slightly elevated from the low-lying land. Rosario remembered the infrared prints he had seen, photos taken from the air which showed the old roads of the Maya.

"There, that road, you see?" Gonzalo pointed. "That leads to the village. At that village there is a large cenote, a natural reservoir of fresh water.... You see, that's why they came! The gods needed the fresh water of the cenotes, they came in great ships to the village, fresh water for their ships...."

His eyes held Rosario spellbound. It was true, from the air the peninsula of Yucatán was flat and dark green in the blue water of the Gulf. There was space to maneuver, no mountains. Yes, he thought, the straight roads are like an airstrip, Uxmal was the center of that civilization that communicated with the gods! The outlying villages were near the cenotes, the fresh water. Fresh water to cool God knows what awesome power source. His heart pounded and his temples throbbed. Yes, he nodded and imagined the bright ships hovering in the night sky, giant beacons lighting up the jungle, the prayer of the winter solstice chanted by thousands of natives, the offering which had been raised to the gods...and then he shook his head, held his hands to his ears to shut away the humming sound. Off to his left two vultures flying high over the jungle had broken his hypnotic gaze.

"No," he said vehemently, "I've heard that story...travelers from outer space. I don't believe it!" He pulled away from the old man who stood dangerously close to the edge of the pyramid.

"I've heard all the stories you told the group, including the one about the gods who came from outer space to establish the ancient civilization of the Mayas. Perhaps your European women believe you, but I don't! I've searched for too long to believe simple stories. For years I have searched for the clue, the secret of the Mayan power, and I'll tell you right now, whatever power the ancient Mayas had is dead! The land is dead! There is no power left!"

Rosario trembled, realizing the outburst was aimed not only at the old man, but at himself. It was what he really felt, an inner realization which came welling from within, a truth he had not wanted to face as long as there had been some hope to his quest. Gonzalo's face grew dark and serious, and Rosario was reminded again of the stela of Copán where the visages suggested pale, yellow Chinese faces of the dark past. He drew close to Rosario and clutched his arm.

"Have you been to Pacal's tomb?" he asked.

"Yes," Rosario replied.

"Have you been to Palenque?"

"Yes."

"Do you know of the astronomers of Copán?"

"Yes."

"Do you believe the Pyramid of the Magician, this sacred place we stand on, was built to honor the gods, built in one night by the dwarf magician of Uxmal?"

Gonzalo's voice rose in strange incantation. Rosario shook his head and pulled free. The old man was crazy, he actually believed the legend.

"No!" Rosario said, "Impossible! The damned thing was built by slaves! So were all the other temples and pyramids built by the sweat of slaves!"

It was as if he had slapped the old man in the face. He cringed and Rosario reached out to grab him because he was so near the edge. "You fool," Gonzalo cursed, "you came to look for the source of power of the ancient Mayas and you can't see it."

"Show it to me," Rosario responded.

"I will show you," Gonzalo said softly, "I will show you how a magician can raise pyramids for the gods...."

He looked into the jungle, and for a long time he did not speak. He stood like a statue, a small, brown man peering into the jungle, an ancient Maya feeling the flow of power between the Earth and the Sun and the planets, listening intently as if to a whispered message.

"Where?" Rosario finally asked and broke the spell.

"There," Gonzalo said and pointed, "south of Uxmal, beyond the hacienda Iman, in that jungle is the village which the gods painted yellow. Come, they are waiting for us!" He scampered down the steep steps of the pyramid and Rosario followed him. They left the ruins and followed a dusty path to the hacienda.

"I will show you a pyramid can still be raised," he mumbled as they walked, "the power of the dwarf is alive tonight," he added, but now the mutterings were in a different dialect and Rosario couldn't understand all that he said.

At the hacienda he sought out a hut near the edge of the field of sisal. There they found a man and a woman who appeared to be waiting for them. Two saddled horses stood beneath the shade of a roble tree. Gonzalo signaled with a flick of his hand and the man brought the horses. When Gonzalo and Rosario were mounted the woman stepped forward and handed each man a small bundle of provisions, then the man and woman quickly disappeared into the hut.

"A'ra!" Gonzalo shouted, and the horse reared up as he spurred it forward. They turned south and rode across the fields of sisal, the yucca-like agave which is cultivated for twine throughout the peninsula.

Where are we going? Rosario thought, why am I following this madman? The strange circumstances of the morning, Gonzalo's mad belief, the man and the woman with the horses, the day of the solstice, everything pointed to some event of strange, mysterious importance. Something exciting had come alive, and he wanted to believe, so he would ride with Gonzalo and see where he would lead.

In the fields a farmer and his workers burned brush. Huge, spiraling columns of greasy smoke rose in the air. They worked to clear the fields, chopping slowly at the dark jungle which returned by night to reclaim the cultivated earth. Crumbling stone fences formed the barrier between cultivated land and wild jungle. The horses moved quietly, and Rosario closed his eyes to preserve his energy. From time to time Gonzalo called out, "A'ra! A'ra!" And he sang in Mayan: "Oh, lost island of Atlantis, floating island of the gods."

The oppressive, humid air was heavy and still. No breeze stirred. Nothing seemed to exist except the burning sun which seared the land and the two lonely horsemen. Gonzalo seemed to be unaffected by the heat, but Rosario, parched with thirst, dug into the bundle the woman had given him and found a gut-skin bag, but instead of water it was full of balché, a fermented drink made of honey. He had tasted balché once before, at a ceremony for Chac, the rain god, the offerings had been bowlfuls of balché which the participants drank after the ritual. It had been a pleasant experience, but here in the middle of the hot afternoon Rosario yearned for water, not the sour drink which fell like warm vinegar into his stomach. Its dizzying effect was immediate. He felt numbness in his arms and legs.

"Hurry! We don't want to be late!" Gonzalo shouted.

Late for what? Rosario wondered. "Do you really believe the gods will come?" he shouted back.

Gonzalo laughed. "They will come!"

Overhead, vultures dotted the clear blue sky, giant birds which rode on the heat waves that rose from the torrid, decomposing jungle.

"The village which the gods painted yellow," Rosario shouted, wondering if he understood the phrase correctly because he had only heard it spoken in Mayan. "Could the translation be, the village painted yellow for the gods?"

The old man didn't answer. As the sun dropped like a burning ball into the western horizon the two urged their horses over a break in the stone wall. They moved along the edge of the jungle until Gonzalo spotted a tree marked with a slash of yellow paint. There they found a deer path and entered the jungle. They were immediately swallowed up by the semi-darkness and the sweltering, humid heat. Rosario thought briefly of Dante entering hell, the door beyond which there was no hope, then he shrugged and slumped in the saddle. Perhaps Gonzalo did know something, he thought, and the journey would reveal something new.

They moved down the narrow path which was canopied by trees and bushes and vines. The brambling vines scratched his face and arms, and when Rosario pushed at the overhanging leaves, clumps of stinging red ants fell on him. They swarmed over both man and beast, raising red welts wherever they stung. Gonzalo seemed unaffected. He led the way into the dark labyrinth. On the path snakes slithered out of the way as they rode deeper and deeper into the sunless maze.

"A'ra! A'ra!" Gonzalo shouted from time to time, and he laughed like a man possessed.

"Let's rest!" Rosario called. "Do you know where we are?"

"We go to greet the gods!" Gonzalo answered. "Soon we rest. We burn copal, drink balché. The gods are there already, in the sky. They wait for us to raise a temple in their honor!"

Overhead a low, eerie sound rose and fell, as if a giant creature was breathing in the darkness. The sound became a drone, growing louder as they penetrated the dark jungle.

Rosario rode as if in a trance. Images appeared in the phosphorescent light of the green night. He thought about the cool cantina, cold beer, the pale and lonely women. He heard their voices and thought how simple and full of pleasure their offering of love would be in his cool room, and he cursed himself for having left. And for what? To follow this dwarf of a man into this hell in search of ancient secrets.

The path grew narrower, it branched out into other deer trails, but Gonzalo led unerringly.

Soaked with sweat and gasping for breath they continued their nightmarish journey. Rosa-

rio thought of the time he had run with the Tara-
humaras in their deep canyons to the north, of
the jump from the pole of the voladores when he
had broken two ribs and sprained both ankles,
and of the hunt in the desert with the Yaquis, all
were ceremonies which tested the endurance of
the body, but there was an unexplainable joy of
the spirit in that rigorous punishment.   Now
there was only a deep, brutal pain which made no
sense.

"The gods will find dead men tonight!" he
laughed in the dark, but Gonzalo did not answer.
And so with a fever working its way through his
tortured body he slept, or thought he slept.   He
imagined the ruins of Uxmal...he dreamed of the
astronomers who kept their vigil there, a vigil for
the gods...and he heard again the story of the
dwarf, the enano who had raised the Pyramid of
the Magician in one night....

All of these images were linked to Gonzalo
and to the trek through the jungle, but Rosario's
feverish mind couldn't make the connection
which would allow a clear image to form. Finally,
they came to a small clearing in the path. A small
altar stood beneath a large ceiba tree, a sacred
tree of the Mayas.   Gonzalo dismounted and
walked to the altar. He placed copal in the incense burner and placed it over the small, glowing fire.   Instantly the air was filled with the
sweet smell of copal. The resinous smoke hung
in the still air like a thin, blue veil.

"Come, drink balché, eat machaca," he commanded.

Rosario slipped off his horse and fell to the
ground. His cramped legs wouldn't support him.
He massaged them, then walked slowly and un-
steadily to the altar. He bit savagely into the dry
venison, the first food he had eaten all day, and he
drank the bowl of balché.

"The spirit is offered to the gods," the old man said, "you may eat the flesh." Then he turned and gazed across the clearing. Before Rosario was finished with his meal, the bush parted and three Indians appeared. They wore only loincloths, and in the dim light of the altar fire Rosario saw their bodies were completely covered with a paint or chalk which glowed a pale yellow. He looked closely as the three approached and again remembered the faces on the stela at Copán.

They bowed in front of Gonzalo and greeted him in a formal manner. "It is the time for the gods," Rosario heard them say, "the time for lights."

"It is the time of Ixchel," Gonzalo answered, "the time of Yum Kin.... It is time to raise new pyramids."

Then he turned, pointed at Rosario, and used the Mayan word to mean assistant. The three bowed. What they did next was done very deftly and quickly. Sharp knives cut away pants and shirts, a cloth was slipped around their loins, and they were covered with the same yellow dust which colored the Indians. It was all done very smoothly, as if they had done it many times before. Gonzalo stood quietly, a willing participant in the ceremony, and Rosario had no time to be surprised. The pieces of some mad design were falling into place, they had found the altar in the clearing, the copal smoke was sweet and thick, and the balché made him numb, dizzy, so when the natives motioned for them to follow, he followed obediently. One of the Indians led the way, the other two came behind with the horses; Rosario understood the village was very near. Overhead the droning sound returned, as if helicopters were whirling in the night sky above the canopy of the jungle. The natives called excitedly to each other and the pace quickened.

Rosario gasped and stumbled forward when they entered the clearing of the village. The bright lights hurt his eyes and he squinted. The chanting of the naked, yellow natives rose in the dark. Everywhere huge bonfires crackled and lit up the night, and because everything was painted yellow the light of the fires gave off a bright, phosphorescent glow. Rosario couldn't believe the yellowish color which had suddenly turned the night into eerie day. He looked in awe. The Indians, the huts, the stone fence around the perimeter of the village, even the trees radiated with the yellow substance.

"El enano! El enano!" the natives cried as Gonzalo and Rosario were led through the village to a large field where the priests of the village waited at a crude, thatched hut, the altar where candles and copal burned. It was full of statuary, old pieces gathered by the Indians from the ruins in the area. Rosario recognized an old and weathered Christ on the cross, the last remembrance of a foolish priest who had tried to convert the natives of the village long ago. In the middle of the hut stood a beautifully preserved stela with the figure of Yum Kin carved on it, and all around it rested food offerings. The clay incense burners glowed with copal, and the sweet smoke filled the night air. At the foot of the altar stood the head priest, and on the ground in front of him rested the sacrificial stone. It was a small square stone carved from black volcanic rock, worn smooth with use.

"You have returned, Magician of Uxmal," the priest greeted Gonzalo. All of the attendants bowed. "It is the time of the gods, time to raise a pyramid in their honor."

Gonzalo nodded. He drew his twisted body to its full height. "I have come to practice the old magic, and I have brought my assistant to help

me...." He motioned with his hand and two attendants pushed Rosario forward. Now, for the first
time, the full impact of the old man's insanity hit
Rosario. What they had come through and what
they were now doing was unbelievable, and yet
everything seemed inevitable, and now here was
the incredible scene of the yellow village with
hundreds of natives surrounding the thatched altar and waiting patiently for the drama to begin.
There is a purpose in all of it, he thought, perhaps I have finally come to that first step by which
I will learn the secrets of the ancient Maya. Perhaps all the secrets I have searched for are about
to be revealed to me. He shuddered and bowed
his head, and like the natives, he gave himself
over to the ceremony about to begin.

"It is time to sing!" Gonzalo shouted. "It is
time to pray. We are the people of the gods. We
pray and they hear us, even as they rest in the
bowels of the earth, even as they rest in the heavens. Tonight I will raise a wondrous pyramid for
them, and they will come and visit us as they did
long ago."

There was a murmur of assent as the natives
fell to their knees. These were the words of the
Magician of Uxmal. The priests drew back. Two
young women moved forward, naked virgins offering the Magician and his assistant bowls of the sacred balché. First Gonzalo raised his bowl upward
and offered it to the gods. In ancient Mayan he
told the gods how the people had gathered to
prepare for this most holy of feasts. For three
days they had fasted, tasting only small portions of
machaca and drinking only the sacred balché.
Then he drank, followed by the priests and Rosario. The young women took the empty bowls and
withdrew.

"I am the Magician of Uxmal," Gonzalo sang, "I
light the way for the gods. In the Jungle of the
Jaguar I will raise a pyramid to Yum Kin, Lord of

the Sun. Because you have granted me this magic, I also dare to sing to Itzamná, the Lord of Life himself...."

This is what he sang, as his voice and the chorus of the people filled the night. Rosario also sang. First he found himself swaying to the rhythmic beat of the chant, and for awhile he was aware of a great loneliness which filled him because he felt himself isolated from the mass of the natives. A sense of responsibility filled him as he glanced at Gonzalo and saw how entranced the old man was in his work. Gonzalo actually believed that he was the Magician of Uxmal, that tonight he would raise a pyramid in the jungle, and the people believed, they sang fervently. Finally, when Rosario closed his eyes and allowed the words of the chant to come pouring out, he too believed it was possible to raise a pyramid in honor of the gods. It could all be done here, tonight, and so he raised his voice and sang.

Deep into the night the chanting continued, the young women returned with bowls of balché, the incense burners were refilled with copal, the fires refueled. Lost Mayan words Rosario had never known tumbled from his lips. A great strength filled him. He felt restored with a faith he had never known, and in his heart he believed that he and Gonzalo were priests, messengers of the gods, men endowed with a special purpose and extraordinary powers. They could raise pyramids to the gods! They could recreate the terrible and ancient mysteries of the past! This is why he had come to the village painted yellow for the gods. This is why he had been chosen, because he had sought and now he of little faith was restored. He felt the power course through his blood and he raised his voice, calling for the pyramid to rise from the empty jungle. At that moment a great wind swirled down and swept up sparks and ashes from the fire. The people cringed with fear then fell prostrate on the ground. Even the priests drew back before the released power.

"There," Gonzalo cried. "There the Pyramid of the Magician rises!"

A shrill, hovering sound came with the wind, the sparks rained on the people and they fled screaming. Out of the swirling, blinding dust a shaft of light broke through and for a moment the image of a golden pyramid shone before their eyes. The earth seemed to shake. Rosario cried in praise then fell to the earth exhausted. The tremendous pain and joy of the night had suddenly drained away and left him empty. Somewhere in the excitement of the moment he heard himself laughing.

He didn't know how long he lay there, but when he looked up he saw the first light of dawn. The air was quiet. Birds called and sang in the jungle. In the southwest the moon was setting over Palenque. He turned and looked at Gonzalo. The old man stood with head bowed, his arms hung limply at his sides. Rosario tried to speak, but no words came.

"You have failed," he heard the priest murmur, but Rosario didn't believe they had failed.

"Next year," Gonzalo nodded, "next year...." He looked at Rosario and his eyes were brilliant and burning. Rosario nodded. He took a step forward to touch his master, but already the attendants had pulled Gonzalo back and bent him over the sacrificial stone. His heaving rib cage stood exposed to the priest who raised the knife.

A glint of the rising sun caught in the sharp obsidian knife as the priest bent over Gonzalo. There was a short gasp for air, a gurgle, and when the priest raised his arms he held Gonzalo's still beating heart in his hands. He held it towards the rising sun, then he dropped the throbbing heart into the altar fire. The people murmured a prayer of thanksgiving.

Gonzalo had not cried out. It was something he seemed to expect. Like a ballplayer in the ball court at Uxmal, he had lost a game, now he was closer to the gods. But Rosario did scream and struggle when the attendants turned on him. It wasn't his heart they wanted. They held him tightly while the priest cut. The cut was swift and sharp, he hardly felt the pain, but when they released him and he tried to stand he fell forward. They had cut his Achilles tendon, they had made him a cripple. He stumbled forward and they parted to let him pass. The searing pain ran up his leg, he was barely able to crawl to the horses. No one moved to stop him. When he reached the staked horses he pulled himself up and mounted while the people only watched. He turned and looked at them and for a moment he saw the truth of the ancient expectations written in their eyes. They had made him their new dwarf, the new magician. A year hence, when the day of the solstice came again to the Yucatán peninsula, he would return, he would be here. This was the time of the Maya, the time of cycles which not even the momentous earth changes nor the cultural changes of centuries could destroy. There was some power yet left to do the work of the gods. He looked across the gathered people, dazzling gold in the bright rays of the morning sun. Yes, now he understood his destiny.

He raised his arm in salute and shouted, "A'ra! Splendor to the Maya!" Then he spurred his horse and rode into the jungle.

SALOMON'S STORY
from the novel *TORTUGA*

THE CHRISTMAS PLAY
from the novel *BLESS ME, ULTIMA*

EL VELORIO
from the novel *HEART OF AZTLAN*

Other stories in this collection have appeared in:

ESCOLIOS
VOICES FROM THE RIO GRANDE
ROCKY MOUNTAIN MAGAZINE
GRITO DEL SOL
HISPANICS IN THE UNITED STATES
and
MOTHER JONES

The author

RUDOLFO A. ANAYA

A native of New Mexico, with an advanced degree in literature from the University of New Mexico at Albuquerque, Rudolfo A. Anaya enjoys an international reputation as an author. Among his writings is the best-selling novel *BLESS ME, ULTIMA*, as well as essays, articles, reviews and short stories. More recently, the creative impulse has led Mr. Anaya into television writing with a screenplay, as well as a full-length drama. He has lectured at many universities, among them Yale, Notre Dame, Texas, Colorado, UCLA and Washington. He has performed as literary judge for the National Endowment for the Arts.

By Presidential invitation, he read from his works at the White House during the National Salute to American Poets and Writers in 1980. He was awarded the Honorary Degree of Doctor of Humane Letters at the University of Albuquerque, and he is the recipient of the New Mexico Governor's Award for Public Service. In California, he has been recognized by the City of Los Angeles for his outstanding achievements and contributions to contemporary American culture.

His novel, *BLESS ME, ULTIMA*, won the Premio Quinto Sol, a national award for best literary work in a national competition.

Book layout and design

Octavio I. Romano-V.

Typesetting by:

TQS PUBLICATIONS